THE SHOP

ON

PECULIAR HILL

written by

GRIMLY DARKWOOD

Cover Illustration by Pete Lyon

Journey
Fiction

Published by Journey Fiction
Las Vegas, Nevada
www.journeyfiction.com

ISBN 978-1-946892-16-4

Library of Congress Control Number: 2018964039

This is a work of fiction. All characters are creations of the author's imagination. Any resemblance to actual persons, living or dead, is coincidental.

Cover illustration by Pete Lyon

18 19 20 21 22 24   6 5 4 3 2 1

ACKNOWLEDGMENTS

For Chris
(who might have preferred
something less peculiar)

With thanks to
Jo and Gareth Webster,
Peter Bortlik,
Naomi and Owen Collick,
and
to Stephen Webster for the nudge that
got things started

Appreciation to Nic Farey and Graham James
for their serendipitous services

Special thanks to
Eric Brown for his encouragement
and
Jennifer Farey for embracing the Strange

1

Peculiar Hill

Peter came to live at Aunt Maggie's shop after his parents were kidnapped by pirates and eaten by tigers, and the Overseers of Children decided the lad was too young to live in the hut on Evil Island without them. Peculiar Hill was not exactly safe—not by the standards of Manchester or Basingstoke, for instance— but the Overseers ruled that it had the edge over Evil Island, being very impressed with the absence of any crocodiles.

So, Peter moved in with his aunt and uncle, arriving one day with a trunk full of all his belongings, except for his hat which was stuffed in a hole in the wall of the hut on Evil Island, to keep out the rain and the pirates.

"We'd better get you a new hat," said Uncle Bob as he lifted the trunk onto the back of the cart at Strange Station, with a bit of help from the Station Master, who didn't have much else to do as this was summer and there weren't many tourists around. Uncle Bob was a big man with a friendly face and a bulging belly. His skin was tanned and leathery, like a well-worn pair of shoes. "You'll need a hat here when the weather turns cold," he explained.

"That's right," said the Station Master. "You'll need a hat here when the bogeys start flying around. Otherwise your head'll get covered in fizz."

Peter climbed up into the cart beside Uncle Bob.

"What are bogeys and fizz?" he asked. He had never heard of such things.

Uncle Bob glared at the Station Master. "You'll find out soon enough, Peter," he muttered, then took the reins to encourage the mules up the hill.

Aunt Maggie was standing at the door of the shop when the cart drew up, next to a large sign saying, "Mules for hire." She had a welcoming smile on her face and a long pole in her hand. She was thin and wiry with pale skin and bulging eyes like a fish. She kept twitching and peering about anxiously.

"You must be Peter," she called out, as the lad climbed down from the cart, then she gave him a sloppy kiss on the cheek and pointed at the sky.

"You see up there?" she asked.

"Yes," said Peter.

"That's the sky," said Aunt Maggie. "That's where bogeys come from and don't you forget it."

"Don't you go and worry the lad," said Uncle Bob. "It's not as dangerous round here as you seem to think." And he took down the trunk and it slipped and fell on top of him.

"Let that be a lesson to you," said Aunt Maggie, when they had called out the next-door neighbours and got the trunk off Uncle Bob with a system of ropes and pulleys. "Don't you go and tell the lad that it's safe round here, 'cos it's not. Not unless you take the proper precautions." She turned her bulging eyes upon Peter. "You see that pole?" she said. "I always keep that pole handy in case I need it for fending off great big bogeys."

"But the bogeys don't fly till November," Uncle Bob protested, "and it's not even July till a week on Tuesday,"

"You can't be too careful," Aunt Maggie said sternly, rolling out a large bandage to put on Uncle Bob. "Now, where does it hurt most?"

When Uncle Bob was bandaged up, they pulled the trunk into the shop. Inside, it was quite dark, but Peter ould see that the walls were covered with row upon row of shelves, crammed full with tins and cans and packets of stuff. Some of these he knew well enough, like baked beans and corn flakes, but others had small, handwritten labels which Peter could hardly read. One tin had a picture of a creature with large wings, cruel little eyes, and great big, sharp teeth, and Peter wondered if this was one of the flying bogeys that everybody was talking about. He rather hoped it wasn't. He stooped closer to try to read the label: "**Aunt Maggie's Home-Made Glop** - *Regular use keeps bogeys at bay. Always read the instructions*".

Uncle Bob was opening Peter's trunk. "Let's see what you got in here," he said, and he and Aunt Maggie started taking out Peter's things.

"He's got no pole for the bogeys," cried Aunt Maggie.

"He's got no hat for their fizz either," said Uncle Bob.

Aunt Maggie muttered something under her breath and it seemed to Peter that she might have been saying a prayer.

"You won't survive round here very long," said Aunt Maggie, "not without a pole for the bogeys and a hat for their fizz and a pair of boots to guard against the heeble-greebs. Didn't you have any things like that on Evil Island?"

Peter had never heard of bogeys or fizz or heeble-greebs, let alone come across them himself, so he shook his head.

"Then I'm not surprised your parents got eaten," said

Aunt Maggie, in a tone which suggested it served them right. "Your Uncle Bob and I would be eaten as well if we didn't take proper precautions."

"Now don't you go and worry the lad," said Uncle Bob. "It's not as dangerous round here as you seem to think." And the door to the shop swung suddenly open and hit Uncle Bob on the part they had bandaged first because it hurt the most.

"I was just saying," said Aunt Maggie, handing Uncle Bob a piece of cloth to stick in his mouth to stifle his cries so they didn't disturb the canary, "we wouldn't survive very long without proper precautions."

"Very true, Mrs. Arkenthrobb," said a thin, wizened man who had entered the shop. "That's a nasty old sneeze you got there," he told Uncle Bob. "Stuck halfway up your nose, is it?"

"He's not sneezing, he's crying out in pain," Aunt Maggie explained, "and he keeps on saying it isn't dangerous round here."

"That's a mistaken belief is that," said the wizened man, stepping forward and standing on Uncle Bob's big toe, which was the bit they had bandaged second because it hurt the second most. "I'll have a bottle of unge please, Mrs. Arkenthrobb," he continued, "and a can of glop and a packet of liquorice all-sorts."

"There you are," said Aunt Maggie. "Mr. Grimble needs unge and glop. If it wasn't dangerous, he wouldn't need stuff like that to protect him, now would he?"

"Just getting set for the winter," said the man she had called Mr. Grimble. "After all, it's July a week on Tuesday."

"What are unge and glop?" asked Peter.

"Well..." began Aunt Maggie.

"Don't tell him, Maggie!" said Uncle Bob, removing the rag from his mouth at last, the worst being over for now. "It's too much for one day, what with the travelling and all. I'll tell him tomorrow when he's had chance to get used to his new home. He's not going to die overnight, now is he?"

Aunt Maggie said nothing, but she and Mr. Grimble exchanged glances and shook their heads in a worried sort of way.

"Well," said Mr. Grimble, turning to Peter. "It was very nice to meet you – I hope we shall meet again."

But he looked as though he feared this might never happen.

2

Aunt Maggie's Lucky Day

"Did you have a good night?" asked Uncle Bob, when Peter came down for breakfast the next day.

"Yes," said Peter, sitting down at the table and helping himself to a slice of toast. He peered doubtfully into a nearby dish. The stuff inside it was lumpy and yellow and looked as though it might glow in the dark.

"Is this supposed to be marmalade?" he asked.

"No, that's a bowl of unge," said Uncle Bob. "The marmalade's in that jar over there, the one with the cross on the top. Turn it three times widdershins before you open it up."

"Turn it three times *what*-ershins?" Peter asked.

"*Widdershins*," said Uncle Bob. "Some folks call it 'anticlockwise' but we call it 'widdershins' here on

Peculiar Hill."

"Why's that?"

"I'll explain later," said Uncle Bob. "Now, are you sure you slept all right?"

"Yes," said Peter, turning the jar three times round and helping himself to some marmalade. His bedroom was a little small and all the cobwebs made him sneeze, but as soon as he'd got used to the spiders it had been all right, he supposed.

"Nothing hovering outside your window or anything like that?" asked Uncle Bob, in the sort of voice he might have used if he had been asking if Peter had enough pillows.

"Not that I noticed," said Peter.

"Good," said Uncle Bob. "And no flashing lights in the sky or strange little scuttling sounds in the skirting boards? Nothing whooping and howling outside your door?"

As he spoke, Uncle Bob pretended to study his fingernails very closely.

"No," said Peter, "nothing like that – not that I can remember."

"And no hideous screeching sounds and nothing lying in bed beside you, all wet and hairy and growling from time to time?"

Peter thought very carefully. "I don't think so – not apart from the spiders."

"That's good," said Uncle Bob, suddenly relaxing. "Much as I thought, really. Now, your aunt and I have decided that after breakfast, I should have a little chat with you about some of the things you might find here on Peculiar Hill that you might not have come across on Evil Island."

"Like unge and glop and bogeys and fizz and heeble-greebs?" asked Peter, taking another mouthful of toast.

Uncle Bob looked uncomfortable.

"Er, yes," he said, "only…"

"Only what, Uncle Bob?"

"Only, well, you don't really need to know *everything*, Peter, not a young lad like you. I don't want to go putting funny ideas in your head…"

"What do you mean, Uncle?"

"I don't want to scare you and make you want to take too many precautions."

"But Aunt Maggie…"

"Aunt Maggie…" Uncle Bob began. Then he looked around and leaned forward and lowered his voice. "Aunt Maggie is working in the shop at the moment. Otherwise, she'd be here now and telling you this herself, but I can't help but think it's lucky it's me instead."

"Why's that, Uncle Bob?"

"Because your aunt is someone who takes too many precautions."

"Like what, Uncle?"

Uncle Bob peered round again. Then he leaned forward even further and whispered under his breath.

"Like never going out of the house – except on a Thursday."

Peter had to admit that this seemed unusual.

"Why's that, uncle?" he asked.

"She once found a five pound note on a Thursday," Uncle Bob explained. "So she says it's her lucky day. Myself, I prefer Fridays. I once dropped a piece of toast on a Friday and it landed butter-side up."

"But what about all the other days of the week?"

"The other days, it always lands butter-side down, but I try to remember to drop it before I put on the butter."

"No," said Peter, "what I mean is, why does Aunt Maggie never go out on the other days of the week?"

"Ah well," said Uncle Bob, "that's 'cos she thinks it isn't safe. And that's where she's wrong, you see."

"Then it's really safe after all, is it?"

"Well," said Uncle Bob, pouring himself a cup of tea. "One thing is certain: it's not as dangerous round here as your Auntie Maggie seems to think." And the lid came off the pot of tea and it poured all over his hand. Peter gave him a napkin to stick in his mouth to stifle his cries, Aunt Maggie having explained about trying not to alarm the canary.

"Thakk yeurr," said Uncle Bob, sounding rather muffled on account of the napkin.

"So you think Aunt Maggie's wrong to stay in all the time?" asked Peter.

"I do." Uncle Bob took the napkin out of his mouth, the worst being over for now. "Because it's not exactly safe outside, but neither is it inside. There's no escape from danger on Peculiar Hill."

Peter must have looked rather alarmed, because Uncle Bob was quick to explain what he meant.

"The way I would put it is this," he said, "it's nowhere near as dangerous as your..." Then he stopped and looked around nervously. "Perhaps I should put it another way, now I think about it. There's danger here on Peculiar Hill but nothing to get upset about – not as long as you take all the right precautions."

"Like putting a bowl of unge on the table and turning the marmalade three times round before you open the jar?" asked Peter.

"Good lad," said Uncle Bob. "That's the sort of thing –

that and a few other sensible measures should see you safe enough."

"Sensible measures like what?"

"That's what I want to tell you about," said Uncle Bob. "I'll just get myself bandaged up and then take you to my study."

B
STRANGE TOMATOES

Uncle Bob's study was at the top of a staircase which Peter hadn't noticed before. This was because it was hidden behind a bookcase.

"There's things up here I like to keep secret," Uncle Bob explained.

"Something to do with the unge and the glop?" asked Peter, climbing the stairs and finding himself in a room with a sloping ceiling, a room which was just as cluttered with stuff as his bedroom was with spiders.

"No," said Uncle Bob, "nothing to do with them at all, nor with bogeys and heeble-greebs. This is where I keep my prize tomatoes." And he opened a cupboard which seemed to have the sun itself inside, so bright was the light which came out of it.

"Wow." Peter shielded his eyes against the glare from the cupboard.

"I just replaced the batteries," Uncle Bob explained.

"It was getting a little dim the other day."

"It's very bright now," said Peter, screwing up his eyes and doing his best to peer inside. "Are there really tomatoes in there?"

"Are there tomatoes?" Uncle Bob sounded rather offended. "These are the finest tomatoes in all the district, I'll have you know. There's people would kill for these tomatoes – that's why I have to keep them hidden. No one else will see them till Strange Show."

Peter asked what Strange Show was.

"The finest agricultural show you'll ever see," said Uncle Bob. "People bring their vegetables from far and wide to Strange Show, all trying to win one of the prizes."

"Do you get a prize for having the largest vegetables?"

"They give prizes for three things," said Uncle Bob, "size, taste, and strangeness. My tomatoes won cups for taste and strangeness last year."

"How do you mean 'strangeness' exactly?" asked Peter.

"Ah well," said Uncle Bob, "that touches on the things I wanted to tell you about. Things round here can often get a bit strange, you see."

"Like bogeys and heeble-greebs, you mean?"

"Well, those are rather extreme examples," said

Uncle Bob. "Other things are more normal, only different."

Peter said he wasn't sure what this meant.

"Take tomatoes, for instance," said Uncle Bob. "Now hang on, I'll just turn out these lights a moment." He pressed a switch and the lights in the cupboard went out. It was like a cloud passing over the sun, and Peter had to blink to adjust to the level of light again. Then he heard mournful wailing from inside the cupboard. He peered closely but could only see tomatoes. They were rather large tomatoes and there were lots of them – all growing inside the cupboard, closely packed together.

"What's that wailing?" asked Peter.

"That's the tomatoes," said Uncle Bob, in a satisfied sort of way. "They don't like it, you see. They didn't like me turning out the light."

Peter could hardly believe it. "That's the tomatoes? But I never..."

"That's what I mean by *strange*," said Uncle Bob. "The judges should give me lots of marks for that. Now listen to this..."

He stretched out a hand and gently stroked one of the nearest tomatoes. It made a loud purring sound.

Peter gave a gasp.

"Just like a cat, ain't it?" said Uncle Bob. "The judges

will give me marks for that as well. I'm hoping to win the strangeness prize for the whole show this year. I'm going for all three tomato cups and 'Strangest Vegetable' too. Mr. Grimble reckons he's got some very peculiar carrots in that garage of his, but I suspect my tomatoes are stranger."

Peter stared in wonder into the cupboard. Had that purring sound been real?

"Can *I* have a go?" he asked.

"Of course you can," said Uncle Bob. "Just make sure you're gentle. It's easy to damage tomatoes if you're rough with them. Just remember, you're petting them, not trying to make soup."

Peter reached out and gently rubbed a finger across the skin of one of the tomatoes. He heard it purr and felt a slight vibration, but when he stopped, he could only hear the wailing again.

"I'd better get these lights switched on." Uncle Bob flicked the switch and closed the cupboard door as the sun came out again inside. "If they go too long without light, the tomatoes might take harm. I don't want Mr. Grimble walking off with the grand prize."

"Er, about this 'strangeness'..." said Peter.

"Yes?"

"How does it happen? How do things get strange?"

"Ah well," said Uncle Bob. "That's a very good question, and just the sort of thing I was going to tell you about. I don't suppose you had anything strange on Evil Island, did you?"

Peter thought very carefully. There were pirates and sharks and crocodiles, of course. And jellyfish and poisonous eels and the odd exploding coconut...but nothing *strange*, exactly.

"No," said Peter, "not really."

"I thought not," said Uncle Bob, looking rather satisfied. "That's why we're so famous round here. Because of the strangeness, you see. That's why so many tourists come to look at The Vale of Strange."

"Where's that?" asked Peter.

"Just at the top of Peculiar Hill. Turn left at The Strange Hotel and you're there."

"And what does it look like, this Vale of Strange?"

Uncle Bob scratched his chin. "I don't really know for certain," he said. "I ain't never seen it."

4

A Perfectly Good Holiday

P eter was puzzled.

"So, this 'Vale of Strange' is just at the top of the hill," he said, "but you don't know what it looks like?"

"Er, well, I know it looks like a vale," said Uncle Bob. "That's a kind of old-fashioned word for a valley, you see."

"But you've never actually seen it?"

"No."

"Not even once?"

"Certainly not," said Uncle Bob. "Seeing it once might be once too many."

"Why's that?" asked Peter.

"It's obvious if you think about it," said Uncle Bob. "If you go and look in The Vale of Strange, you'll see all the strangeness there, and that can only mean one thing."

"What's that?" asked Peter.

Uncle Bob leaned over so that his face was close to Peter's. He narrowed his eyes and spoke in a sort of croak.

"If you can see all the things that are strange, they'll be able to see you—all the bogeys and heeble-greebs and other things like ghosts and stuff—and you can't never say where that might lead, Peter."

"What do you mean?" Peter found that he was whispering too, without knowing why.

"Ah, well, it could be very dangerous, you see. Some of those creatures are fierce. After all, you know what happens to tourists..."

"No," said Peter, "I don't."

"Ah no," said Uncle Bob, "I don't suppose you do. And I reckon it's better if you *don't* know, now I think about it."

Suddenly, Peter was very eager to know what happened to tourists.

"Oh, go on, Uncle Bob, tell me,"

"Not now, I don't think, Peter. It'll be too much to take in, what with the travelling and all. And besides which, we don't always *know* what happens to tourists, not all of them anyway. We don't always find the bodies."

Peter gasped. "You mean...?"

"No, no," said Uncle Bob. "I'm giving you the wrong idea. It's not like that at all. Most tourists who come to The Vale of Strange have a perfectly good holiday."

"Except that...?"

"Except that, well, some of them don't return. I think that's the best way of putting it. Yes. Some of them don't return."

"And why is that?" asked Peter.

Uncle Bob peered about wildly, as though he was trapped and looking for some way out.

"Well... I... What I mean is... Look," he said at last, "we're looking at this the wrong way round. Most tourists find their trip extremely entertaining. It's something they can talk about for many years to come. Why, it might be the best holiday some of them ever have."

"I suppose it might be," Peter muttered, "if it turns out to be their last."

Uncle Bob became rather annoyed at this.

"Now, Peter, I'm surprised at you. I don't think you're really listening to what I'm saying. It's very important, so pay attention, all right? The Vale of Strange is one of the finest tourist attractions in the whole world. That's why the government spends so much money promoting it— so that everyone gets to hear about it and gets the chance to go. Why, people who can't afford to go can even get financial assistance. That means the government gives them money to make the trip. The Vale of Strange is that special, you see."

"Why is it special?" asked Peter.

"Because it's spooky," said Uncle Bob, "because of all the strange creatures that don't live anywhere else. Haven't you seen the brochure?"

"No, I haven't."

"Ah, no, I don't suppose you have, what with you living abroad and all. Hang on a moment, I'll get you one."

He turned round and rummaged amongst some clutter. As he searched, various tools and tin cans and something that looked like a trumpet fell on the floor. "I think your Aunt Maggie's been tidying up in here again," he complained. "I can't never find nothing when she does that. Ah, wait a minute...here we are, There's one here under this fish..."

He brought out a leaflet and handed it to Peter.

"The Vale of Strange," read Peter, "a spine-chilling adventure. Explore this spooky, natural valley, full of extraordinary creatures. Good for holidays. Great for picnics. Government recommended."

In the centre of the leaflet was a picture of a flying creature like the one which Peter had seen the previous day on the can of glop. It looked just as fearsome on the brochure as it had before.

"Is that a bogey?" asked Peter.

"Yes," said Uncle Bob. "That's a bogey, all right. But don't worry—they don't go flying about until October."

Peter was trying to understand what was going on.

"So, tourists come to The Vale of Strange, which is full of bogeys and other creatures…"

"That's right. Like heeble-greebs and stuff."

"But aren't they afraid that the creatures will kill them?"

"No," said Uncle Bob. "No, they're not."

"But you've already said that some of the tourists never return," said Peter. "The creatures there are so dangerous that you've never been to the vale yourself, and it's only up at the top of Peculiar Hill. Aren't the tourists worried about the danger too?"

"No," said Uncle Bob, "I told you, they aren't worried at all."

"Why's that?" asked Peter.

Uncle Bob looked very uneasy. He cleared his throat before he replied. "Because nobody tells them about it."

5

Aunt Maggie Makes Glop

"Bob!" shouted Aunt Maggie from down below. "It's time you were getting up to the hotel."

Uncle Bob gave a gasp and looked at his watch.

"Oh, is that the time?" he said. "I didn't know it was getting so late, and I haven't had chance to tell you much about what to look out for round here. Still, never mind, eh? I'll have more time tomorrow and I don't suppose you'll die overnight, now will you?"

Peter said he would do his best to stay alive but was very curious even so to hear all the things that Uncle Bob had to tell him.

"Could I ask Aunt Maggie? Will she have time to tell me while she's working in the shop?"

"No," said Uncle Bob, looking panic-stricken. "You mustn't ask Aunt Maggie. She'll tell you more than you need to know and be giving you nightmares. You have to promise me, Peter. Promise me you won't go and ask Aunt Maggie."

Uncle Bob stared fixedly at Peter, and it didn't seem to Peter that he had any choice but to agree.

"All right, Uncle Bob," he muttered, though he'd never made a promise he felt less like keeping.

"Bob!" came Aunt Maggie's voice again, more urgently this time.

"Coming, Maggie!" called Uncle Bob. "We'll be down in just a tick!"

As they left the study, Peter looked wistfully at all the stuff piled around its walls and on every spare shelf and every inch of table. There were boxes and tins and ornaments and odd contraptions with knobs and dials; books and papers and rusty tools; models of trains and aeroplanes, and something that looked like a bicycle built for a man with too many legs. Some of it looked as interesting as the strange purring, wailing tomatoes, and Peter would have liked to stay and take a closer look.

"We'll come back here for a root about another time," said Uncle Bob, who had noticed Peter's expression and guessed what he was thinking. "I'll show you the peculiar clock, and the wild and wacky sausage machine, and the very curious can of baked beans."

"You haven't even told me how things get strange,"

Peter complained.

"I'll tell you tomorrow." Uncle Bob drew aside the bookcase at the bottom of the stairs. "Now don't go letting on to Aunt Maggie that you still don't know very much, will you?" he whispered. "You'll get me into trouble if you do."

"All right," said Peter very reluctantly. He didn't think that Uncle Bob was being very fair, but he wanted to see the peculiar clock, the wild and wacky sausage machine, and the very curious can of baked beans, so he thought he should tell Uncle Bob what he wanted to hear.

"Have you told him?" asked Aunt Maggie, as they walked into the shop. She was filling up some cans of glop, ladling the stuff with a spoon out of a large, bubbling vat which was cooking over a fire. The glop was red and sticky, like thick tomato soup. It smelt like disinfectant mixed with strawberries.

"Yes, I've told him," said Uncle Bob breezily. "That looks like very fine glop you're brewing up there, Maggie. Judging by the whiff of the stuff, it's the best you've ever made."

Aunt Maggie ignored her husband's remarks. "Have you told him about fizz? Does he understand why he needs to wear a hat?" She stared at Peter searchingly, as though she could tell what he knew just by looking.

"Why he needs to wear a hat in *October*, you mean," said Uncle Bob, "not in June, when there aren't any bogeys about."

Aunt Maggie put down her ladle.

"He needs to wear a hat in *September*," she said pointedly, "at the very latest."

"*Late* September," said Uncle Bob, heading for the door. "Come on, Peter. You can come to the hotel and play with Amanda while I'm working."

"He can stay here and help me in the shop if he likes," said Aunt Maggie. "Help me ladle out this glop."

"It looks like you're coping very well on your own, Maggie," said Uncle Bob, pushing Peter out of the door. "See you later, then."

"And does he know about heeble-greebs?" called Aunt Maggie. "Does he know to wear boots and thick trousers and..." Her voice became faint as Uncle Bob slammed the door shut behind them.

"She's right about the heeble-greebs, I suppose." Uncle Bob looked a bit worried as he climbed onto the cart. "The other strange creatures are tucked up snug in The Vale of Strange all summer, but you can get heeble-greebs about at any time of the year. We'd better get you fitted up with some boots when I'm finished at the hotel. Don't go in any long grass in the meantime, now will you,

Peter?"

"No, Uncle Bob," said Peter, climbing onto the cart beside him. "Uncle…"

"Or standing on any thick carpets, neither?"

"Uncle Bob," Peter asked, "who's Amanda?"

6
AMANDA CHUBB

"Amanda's a girl of about your age who lives at The Strange Hotel," said Uncle Bob, as he took the reins to coax the mules up the hill. "Her parents own the hotel, you see. Mr. and Mrs. Chubb. That's where the tourists stay when they come to see the vale."

Peter said he had stayed in hotels himself on the way to Evil Island. They were tall and shiny and full of potted plants.

"Well...this one's a little bit different," said Uncle Bob. "It's more sort of tall and gloomy and full of rats. But the tourists never seem to complain. Not even the ones that survive. Mind you, they've all been through The Sweeper, of course."

"What's The Sweeper?" asked Peter.

Uncle Bob looked uneasy again. "That's what I'm off there to mend. It's broken down again. It's one of those things I'll explain about tomorrow. All you need to know for now is not to go through the hotel door when the light is on, all right? It's very important is that. *Don't go through the hotel door when the light is on.*"

"I mustn't go through the hotel door when the light is on," repeated Peter, who couldn't wait to give it a try to see what happened.

"Good," said Uncle Bob, "'cos that's when The Sweeper's working, you see, when the light is on. And you wouldn't want to be Swept—not like the tourists are. Not that there are many tourists around at this time of year. It's off-season, you see. Not much point in them coming here with most of the creatures asleep."

"About this Sweeper..." Peter began, but then he saw something which took away his breath. A high building had come into view on the left-hand side of the road: big and black and sprouting turrets which looked like enormous mushrooms.

"Is that a castle?" Peter asked when he could breathe again.

"That's the hotel," said Uncle Bob, turning the cart onto a long driveway which led up to the building. "You can see why the tourists like it, in spite of the rats. It's dark and spooky and gets 'em all in the mood for The Vale of Strange."

"Are there bogeys in there?" Peter thought it looked like the sort of place where frightening creatures might live, and as he spoke, something flew out of one of the turret windows. It circled about for a moment or two and then disappeared again.

"That's just a bat," said Uncle Bob. "They're safe enough as long as you don't try to stroke 'em. And as for bogeys, you don't often get 'em here. The precautions they take are very good, you see. They need to be good, so close to The Vale of Strange."

"So, they have lots of unge and glop, do they, and crosses on jars of marmalade?"

"Not only that..." began Uncle Bob, but his words were drowned out by a terrible noise which came from the hotel. It sounded like something had stood on the paws of all the hounds of hell.

"That's the watch-geese," Uncle Bob said, raising his voice above the din. "They keep them up on the battlements here, and very effective they are. They make enough noise to alert Mr. Chubb and send any bogeys back to the vale with their tails between their claws into the bargain. We sell 'em down at the shop, you know, specially bred for extra screechability. Ah, there's Mr. Chubb now."

A man wielding a long pole had appeared at a large

door at the end of the driveway. When he saw Uncle Bob, he put down the pole and approached the cart, beaming all over his face.

"I thought it must be you!" He shouted above the noise of the geese. "All the tourists we've been expecting are already here and the bogeys are still in hibernation. Even so, you can't be too careful so close to the vale. Some of these bogeys can fly around in their sleep,"

"How many tourists you got?" shouted Uncle Bob.

"Only three," hollered Mr. Chubb, "but they'll need Sweeping all the same. The government won't be happy if they don't get a going over." He squinted at the battlements high above. "If those geese don't shut up soon, I'll have to get out the hose and give them a soaking."

"This is Peter," yelled Uncle Bob, introducing his nephew to Mr. Chubb. "I thought that if Amanda's around..."

But Peter had already seen her. She was sitting on the steps leading up to the door. She had long hair and piercing eyes and was looking on intently. When Uncle Bob and Mr. Chubb went off to see to The Sweeper and the watch-geese began to calm down at last, she got to her feet and slowly approached Peter. Something in the way she walked made Peter very wary. She looked as though she was sidling up for a showdown.

"How many bogeys you seen?" she asked, as though this was the way that strangers normally greeted each other – instead of saying "Hello" or "How do you do?"

"Er, none," said Peter lamely.

Amanda pursed her lips. She didn't look as though she was very impressed. "Then what about heeble-greebs?" she asked. "You seen any of them?"

Peter shook his head.

Amanda gave a pitying sigh, as though he'd just confessed that he didn't know how to blow his nose.

"And I haven't seen any fizz either," Peter said quickly, thinking it might be a bit less worse if he got in first this time.

But it didn't make any difference.

"And I don't suppose," said Amanda, speaking as though she was very, very bored, "that you've seen any neeps or shufflebottoms either?"

Peter was more disconcerted than ever. Now there were things he hadn't seen that he hadn't even heard about.

"I've seen crocodiles," he muttered in desperation.

Amanda raised her eyes to the sky. "Everyone's been to the zoo," she cried in disdain.

"But I've seen them out in the real world," Peter

protested.

"Big deal!" said Amanda.

Peter realised he couldn't win at this game. He couldn't impress Amanda unless she was willing to be impressed, and all she seemed to be willing to be was bored.

Peter was getting angry.

"I've only just arrived," he said. "You can't expect me to..."

"What about practical jokes?" asked Amanda. "You played any good ones, have you?" She looked as though she didn't expect that he had.

Peter remembered the time he had tickled the crocodiles with the sweeping brush and then run off before they bit him, but he didn't think it was worth the bother of mentioning. He was sure that Amanda would not be impressed, whatever he said.

He decided to play a different game instead.

"So...you live here with your parents, do you?" he said, sounding aggressive.

His change in tone seemed to catch Amanda off guard.

"Er, yes," she replied uncertainly.

"And the tourists stay here when they come to look at The Vale of Strange?"

"Yes," said Amanda, as though wondering where this was leading.

Peter smirked to himself. He had got her now. He was going to make her feel very, very guilty.

"Then why don't you warn them?" he cried. "Some of those tourists die here, don't they? They die in The Vale of Strange. But you let them stay here and never say a thing!"

There. He had got it said. He stood and waited, expecting to see her look very ashamed of herself.

But to his surprise, it wasn't like that at all.

Her eyes lit up and she gave a broad grin.

"Warn the tourists!" she cried. "I never thought of that. What a brilliant joke! That'll really, really annoy my parents. You're not so bad after all. Come on!" And she grabbed Peter by the hand and pulled him up the steps to The Strange Hotel.

7

WARNING THE TOURISTS

"The tourists are having lunch," said Amanda, "but I know how we can get to them without anyone seeing."

The inside of The Strange Hotel was dark and hung with lanterns. They crossed a large entrance hall and entered a narrow corridor between walls of bare stone. Amanda stopped, looked both ways, and lifted a metal grill off the wall.

"Get inside," she said. "Quickly!"

Peter looked at the hole in the wall and then back at Amanda. He was wondering how he had managed to get himself into this.

"Go on!" said Amanda. "I haven't got all day, you know." She thrust her nose high in the air, as though she were a very important person.

"But..."

"Look, we have to hurry. If we stay here long, my father will come and we'll be found out."

Something in her tone of voice spurred Peter into action. Before he knew it, he'd gone through the hole and was lying flat in a narrow channel inside the wall.

"Budge up!" said Amanda. "Make room for me."

There was so little space inside the channel that Peter was only able to move by pushing with his elbows against the floor. As he moved along, he heard Amanda get in behind him and replace the grill with a clang.

"Where are we?" asked Peter.

"In a central heating duct," said Amanda. "It was built to carry hot air round the building. They had the central heating put in because the hotel's so cold. It cost my parents a fortune, but it doesn't work anymore. Bogeys kept getting stuck in the flues. Can't you move any faster?"

"I'm doing my best," said Peter, who wasn't used to crawling around in central heating systems. They didn't have them on Evil Island. Which just as well, because if they did, they'd probably be full of crocodiles.

"If you don't get a move on, we'll be too late," said Amanda.

"Too late for what?" Peter was feeling a bit grumpy because his elbows were starting to hurt. And it didn't help his mood to hear a sharp intake of breath from just behind him.

"To warn the tourists of course," said Amanda. "Where do you think we're going? I thought this was your idea."

"It wasn't my idea to crawl around on our hands and knees," Peter protested. "I don't see what this has to do with warning the tourists."

"It's like I said, they're having lunch," said Amanda. "We can't just walk up and tell them, or someone will see. But I saw them going into the dining room earlier on and I know they're sitting at table one, and that's got a central heating grill beside it."

Peter began to understand. "So, we're going to climb out of it and...?"

"Of course not!" Amanda snapped. "Are you stupid or something? That'll take ages, especially as slow as you are. All we have to do is call across to them."

Peter found he was crawling past another grill. Looking through the opening, he could see lots of tables with white cloths across them.

"I think we're next to the dining room now," he said.

"Good," said Amanda. "We're almost there. The next grill should be the one we want. Make sure to keep your voice down. We don't want Bletch to hear us, do we?"

"Who's Bletch?" asked Peter.

He heard another sharp intake of breath.

"Don't you know *anything*?" asked Amanda.

"I know how to get milk out of a coconut."

"And how exactly is *that* supposed to help us warn the tourists?"

Peter would have glared at her, but there wasn't any room to turn around.

"Get a move on," Amanda whispered. "They'll soon have finished their lunch."

"You still haven't told me who Bletch is," Peter protested.

"Bletch is my parents' waiter," said Amanda, "and cleaner and clerk and stuff like that. Whatever needs doing, he'll do it, only very, very slowly. He's even slower than you are, but he's old, so he's got an excuse."

"You're always getting at me," said Peter.

"Oh dear," said Amanda, "what a shame!"

Peter was getting very, very angry. "That does it! I'm…"

Then there came a funny noise from farther along the duct.

"Oh no!" Amanda said. "Close your eyes and mouth and put your head down."

"Why?"

"Just do it!" Amanda was so insistent, Peter did what she said.

And a moment later, it happened. With a sudden *whoosh*, a cloud of something black came down the duct. Peter's head felt like it was covered in sticky, powdery goo.

"Was that an attack of fizz?" he asked in a panic.

Amanda sniggered.

"Of course not," she said. "It was just a cloud of soot. That happens from time to time when the wind's in the wrong direction. It's because there's still a bogey trapped in the flue."

"Then why's it sticky?" asked Peter, feeling his face.

"Oh, just bogey stuff," Amanda said dismissively.

Peter wondered what this meant, but Amanda told him to hurry and get a move on.

"Do you really want this to be a wasted journey?" she asked.

Peter certainly didn't—especially not now that he was covered in soot and stuff. He forced his aching elbows to push him forward. They would make it in time, he told himself. After all this, they *had* to get there in time to warn the tourists.

"Only a little bit farther now," said Amanda, and Peter tried to remember if this was the first thing she had said that hadn't annoyed him.

And then he saw a grill ahead to his left.

"It looks like we're almost there," he said.

"Make sure you keep your voice down," Amanda reminded him. "Bletch might be nearby."

One more push and Peter was able to see out through the grill. He could see a table close at hand, and three people sitting around it: a man, his wife, and their son, it seemed to be. These must be the tourists, Peter supposed. And there, standing beside them, was a tall, thin, wrinkled old man in a dark suit and a shirt with a bow-tie. It must be Bletch, the waiter.

"I trust you found the meal to your liking?" Bletch was saying.

Oh no, Peter thought. *We're going to be too late after all! Now they're going to get up and leave and we won't have chance to warn them.*

"The meal was very good," said the man at the table, "but I wonder if you have such a thing as a tooth-pick?"

Bletch bowed very low.

"You shall have one in a moment, sir." He straightened up with difficulty and hobbled slowly off across the room.

It occurred to Peter that Bletch's "moment" might be somebody else's hour. He willed the old man to disappear so it would be safe to call to the tourists.

"What's happening?" Amanda whispered. "What can you see?"

"Bletch was there, but he's going," said Peter. "I wish he'd get a move on,"

"Now you know how I feel about you," said Amanda.

The tourists were sitting talking at the table. The adults had their backs to the grill, so Peter was better able to see the boy. He was quite a few years younger than Peter, with red hair and spectacles and freckles.

Peter looked and saw that Bletch was finally gone. But now that the coast was clear, he didn't know what to say.

"What shall I tell them?" he whispered to Amanda.

He heard that familiar sharp intake of breath.

"How to get milk from a coconut?" she suggested.

"How's that going to...?"

"Don't be stupid. Tell them they're going to die," said Amanda crossly. "But hurry up or Bletch'll be back."

Peter cleared his throat and shuffled around to get comfortable before he shouted the warning. But by mistake, one of his elbows banged against the grill.

"You're all going to..."

Before Peter had hardly started, the boy shrieked and pointed at the grill.

"Bogey!" he cried. "Look—a bogey! It's going to come out and get me."

"...die!" Peter completed his warning, but in his alarm the word might have sounded more frightening then he had intended.

As the adults turned to look at the grill, Peter instinctively backed away, bumping into Amanda.

"Can't you watch where you're going?" she whispered fiercely.

"Of course I can't," said Peter. "I don't have eyes in my–"

"There's nothing there, Algernon," the boy's father was saying. "Besides, all those ghosts and bogeys and things are quite harmless, really. They may look very frightening, but they can't actually hurt you. You remember—you've seen the government film."

"It had a big ugly face," said the boy. "It was horrible."

Peter took exception to this. He moved closer to the grill and glared at the boy.

"There it is again!" cried the boy and he started to sob loudly.

Peter cursed and dodged out of view as Bletch came hobbling back across the room.

"There's nothing there," the father said. "Look... I'll take you over there. Hold my hand. Now, don't be afraid.

No, Algernon—stay here! Come back, Algernon!"

But Algernon was already scurrying towards the door, bawling as he went. "Don't wanna see bogeys! *Waugghhh!*"

"Algernon, dear," his mother cried, "come to Mummy, darling!"

"Algernon! Algernon!" his father shouted crossly. "Come back here, Algernon!"

"Don't forget your toothpick, sir!" called Bletch.

"Quick," whispered Amanda, "let's get out of here."

"But we haven't warned them properly yet," Peter complained.

"That's tough," said Amanda, "but we need to go before Bletch comes across to that table and sees us. He takes ages clearing things up. We'll be stuck here all day. Come on. Get a move on, can't you?"

Reluctantly, Peter began to push himself forward again. There seemed to be a bend in the duct ahead of him.

"Be careful as you–"

But Amanda's warning came too late. Peter turned the corner and suddenly, thanks to a steep downward slope in the duct, his progress was no longer slow. He found himself sliding at an ever-increasing speed down into the unknown depths of The Strange Hotel.

8

FULL STRANGE BREAKFAST

When Peter came to a stop, he found himself in a small, gloomy room, dark except for the faint light which came through an open hatch on the wall ahead. He tried to move but slid around in something soft and sort of gritty. It was like swimming in dry, scratchy water.

"Move out of the way!" came Amanda's voice from behind.

Turning round with difficulty, Peter saw a small opening in the wall, about the size of the channel through which they had crawled. There was no sign of Amanda.

"Where are you?" he cried.

"Here I am!" called Amanda. "Still up here in the central heating duct. If you're careful as you go round the bend, you can wedge yourself with your shoulders and feet so you don't slide down it the way you did. If you hadn't been in such a hurry, I could have showed you."

"You *told* me to get a move on," Peter complained.

"Well, so what? It was fun, wasn't it?"

"Perhaps if I'd been expecting it."

"Well then, get out of the way so I can have a go. If you don't move, I'll do you serious damage."

With new urgency, Peter did his best to move out of the way. He managed to reach the edge of the stuff and climbed over a low wall onto solid ground beyond. It was good to have something predictable under his feet.

"What are you doing down there?" asked Amanda. "Eating it, are you?"

"I don't know what you're talking about," said Peter, rather annoyed, "but it's safe to come down if you want, I suppose."

"All right. Here goes!"

With a squeal of delight, Amanda slid into view, then almost disappeared under the gritty stuff. She thrashed around for a while and then emerged with a grin.

"Good, isn't it?" she said.

Peter stuck his fingers into the stuff, grabbed a handful, and studied it by the light of the hatch.

"It looks like..."

"Yes, that's right. It's porridge oats. This used to be

the boiler room, but now that it's broken they're using it as a porridge store. The kitchen is just upstairs, you see. It's convenient."

Peter gaped at the porridge store in astonishment.

"Do the tourists eat a lot of porridge?" he asked.

"It's traditional," said Amanda. "It's all part of the deal: 'full strange breakfast, complete with piping hot Vale of Strange porridge'. The tourists eat a bowl of it before they go and die."

Peter studied the oats suspiciously. "Is it *strange* porridge?"

"No," said Amanda, "it isn't strange at all. It's not even locally grown, in fact. We get it imported cheap from Singapore. If you want to see something strange, though, I can show you."

Peter felt suspicious. What was this girl going to get him into now?

"I've seen strange tomatoes," he said defensively.

"Strange tomatoes are boring. This is much, much better. Help me out of the porridge oats and I'll show you,"

She led him out through the hatch and up a flight of stairs beyond. At the top of the stairs was a door where she stopped and listened.

"We don't want Bletch or my parents to see us," she

whispered. "They don't like people polluting their porridge oats."

"Then they shouldn't leave them lying around where people are going to slide in them," said Peter.

"Just be glad they hadn't added the hot milk and the treacle. Come on. The coast's clear, I think."

"We used to have salt on our porridge on Evil Island," Peter recalled.

"The tourists have a sweet tooth. We mollycoddle them here at The Strange Hotel. I'll show you how much in a moment." Amanda led him through the door and along a narrow passage beyond. At a junction, they joined a wider, lighter passage with chandeliers. "Here we are!" she declared, and to Peter's horror, she led them through a door marked *Ladies*.

9
GETTING WASHED

"**I** can't come in here." Peter pulled back, but Amanda wouldn't let go.

"Don't be stupid," she said. "Of course you can. There's nobody in here. The tourists will be up in their rooms, getting ready to leave for The Vale of Strange."

"But…"

"Oh, shut up," said Amanda, tugging him through the door. "If you hover around outside like that, someone'll see you."

"But…"

"And you *need* to come in here—or hadn't you noticed?"

"I don't know what you mean," he said, looking around. They were in a vast and very luxurious toilet. The walls and floor were of polished marble, and all along the wall to the right was a row of white washbasins with glittering taps of gold. There was also a faint and rather sickly smell of peaches.

"Look in one of the mirrors then," said Amanda.

Above each of the basins was a fancy mirror with a golden border. Peter turned and peered into the nearest.

"Bliminy!" he cried.

"You see?"

Peter could see now. His whole face and the shoulders and front of his shirt were covered in soot. He remembered the cloud of black stuff which had come along the duct.

"Is this why that boy mistook me for a bogey?" Peter asked. "Do bogeys have black faces then, like this?" He thought of the pictures of bogeys he had seen back at the shop and tried to remember what colour they had been.

"Bogeys don't really look like you at all," Amanda told him. "That tourist just had a vivid imagination. He'd probably heard that some bogeys are black, 'cos some of them are, but others are pale, some are green, and others are covered in red spots as though they have the measles. It all depends what species they are, you see. But if I were you, I'd have a wash, or you're going to be in trouble."

Peter supposed she was right. If Aunt Maggie and Uncle Bob were anything like his parents, getting as dirty as this would have repercussions. He gave a sigh and approached the nearest basin.

"This won't make very much difference," he said. "I'll still have a dirty shirt."

"Stop whining and get washed," said Amanda.

Peter held a hand out flat beneath a nearby soap dispenser and pressed the gilt plunger, expecting a small amount of soap to trickle onto his hand.

But this was where he was very, very wrong.

Without any warning, the soap squirted in vast amounts all over his face and the dirty part of his shirt. For a moment or two, he could hardly breathe. Then he wiped it away from his mouth and eyes as he gasped for air.

"What...?"

Amanda was bent over double with laughter. She seemed to be having trouble breathing too.

"You *knew* that was going to happen," said Peter. "You deliberately..."

"Ha, ha, ha," said Amanda. "Your face!"

Peter looked and saw it was covered in green goo, as was the part of his shirt that was dirty with soot.

"Now I'm in a worse mess than ever," he complained. "I'm going to get some of this goo and..."

"You leave me alone!" said Amanda. "I'm only trying to help. If you don't believe me, take a towel and wipe the soap away."

"But…"

"Look, it's *strange* soap. You wanted to see something strange, didn't you? Well now you have." She handed him a paper towel. "Take that and wipe it away. Then you'll see what I mean."

Peter took the towel with great suspicion. What trick was Amanda going to play next, he wondered? But he wiped his face and then looked in the mirror. To his great surprise, his face was entirely clean. He felt it with his other hand. It wasn't even sticky.

"Now your shirt," said Amanda.

Still not entirely trusting, Peter wiped the shoulders and front of his shirt, but it came up brilliant white as though it had just come out of the washer.

"Bliminy!" he cried.

Amanda stood there grinning.

"Good, isn't it? It automatically squirts itself onto the bits of you that are dirty. Then you just wipe it away and you're clean."

"And this is strange soap?"

"Yep."

"So why doesn't Aunt Maggie use it?" asked Peter.

Amanda started to smile.

"Ah, well…" she said, looking secretive.

Peter gave her a look.

"All right, I'll tell you," she said. "Only the tourists use it. I don't use it and neither do Bletch or my parents."

Peter was getting a bad feeling about this.

"And is there some reason for that?" he asked with narrowed eyes.

Amanda twisted her face into a funny sort of expression. "Um, yes," she said, trying not to laugh.

"What is it, Amanda?" asked Peter, raising his voice slightly. "What have you made me do?"

"Well, how else were you going to get clean?" asked Amanda.

Peter glared.

Amanda gave a shrug.

"In a few days, your shirt will start to disintegrate," she said. "There. That wasn't so bad, was it?"

Peter's expression suggested that it might be.

"That's why we leave it out for the tourists, you see," Amanda explained. "They think the stuff is really great, and by the time their clothes fall apart, they're gone."

Even Peter could see this was sort of funny, not that he'd admit it to her.

"But *I* won't be gone," he protested, "and neither will Aunt Maggie,"

"Oh, don't worry about her," said Amanda. "She'll just

think there's a problem with her washing machine."

Peter looked in the mirror again to check that his face was still there. It seemed to be intact, but he looked at Amanda quizzically all the same.

Amanda gave a sigh. "Don't worry. Your precious face is safe. Only your shirt is destined to die. Trust me."

"Trust *you*?" cried Peter. "Why should I trust *you*? With all the tricks you like playing, I don't see why I should ever believe a word you say."

To his surprise, Amanda looked rather hurt.

"I'm only trying to have a bit of fun," she said. "There's not much fun at The Strange Hotel, not when you're all alone here except for your parents and Bletch. Not when none of your friends from school dare to come and play with you because you live so close to The Vale of Strange."

All of a sudden, Peter felt rather bad.

"Oh, I see. I..."

Amanda's eyes glistened slightly, but then she brightened again and started to dance in twirls around the ladies' room.

"I like to pretend it's a ballroom," she said, "like on the old films. It's very splendid, don't you think? I told you we mollycoddle the tourists. All this and strange soap as well. Even the toilets are strange, you know. I'd show you, but it wouldn't really be proper."

"But some of the tourists are going to die!" Peter kept on coming back to this. Amanda's jokes were all very well, but this was a serious business.

"But all the tourists who come away have enjoyed themselves," said Amanda.

"What, even if they've left one of their friends or relatives dead in the vale behind them? I bet the ones that have done that don't enjoy themselves very much."

"They all come away and say they've had a lovely time," said Amanda. "You can ask your Uncle Bob if you don't believe me."

Peter suddenly wondered if Uncle Bob had finished his work.

"Do you think he'll have fixed that—what was it? The Sweeper?—yet?"

Amanda paused and thought for a moment. Then she looked as though she'd had an idea.

"We can go and see if you like," she said brightly. "Come on!" And she led Peter out of the door of the ladies' room and up a splendid flight of stairs which brought them back to the entrance hall. But there wasn't any sign of Uncle Bob.

"Do you want to see if he's waiting outside?" asked Amanda.

"All right," said Peter, walking towards the door. And then he heard Amanda's snigger behind him. If it hadn't been for that, he would not have remembered. But he looked and saw the light above the door.

He turned round very slowly to glare at his companion.

"Ah," she said, looking disappointed. "They've told you about it then, have they? What a shame!"

10

THE SWEEPER

"Uncle Bob told me not to go through the entrance door when the light was on," said Peter, "but *you* were just going to stand there and watch me, weren't you?" Admittedly, when he'd first heard about the light, he'd wanted to go through the door anyway, just to see what happened, but after all the adventures he'd had since he'd come to The Strange Hotel, he decided he'd had enough surprises for one day. So he glared at Amanda, feeling very annoyed.

Amanda smiled. "It wouldn't have been so bad. All that happens when you go through the door is your eyes pop out and your mouth furs up and your brain turns to raspberry jelly. It's quite fun, if you like that sort of thing."

Peter tried to decide if she was lying.

"I think you're lying," he said.

Amanda gave a shrug.

"Maybe," she said, "maybe not, but there's one good

way to find out. Go through the door yourself and prove me a liar,"

"I could push *you* through instead," said Peter.

"Bully!" said Amanda. "Anyway, I've been through once already. I'd find it very boring to do it a second time."

"Now you're lying again," said Peter.

"No, I'm not. I told you it gets very dull. One afternoon, there was nothing else I could think of to pass the time."

Peter decided he almost believed her now.

"Then you must have been lying before," he said. "Your eyes haven't popped out."

"I didn't say they wouldn't grow back again, did I?"

"And what about your brain turning to jelly?"

Amanda thought for a moment. "As long as you eat the strawberry jelly, your brain grows back as well."

"Ha! Caught you!" Peter cried. "You said it was *raspberry* jelly before."

Amanda pursed her lips. "It depends on the time of year. Whatever fruit's in season."

Peter gaped in astonishment. Was there no defeating this girl?

Amanda's face lit up in a smile of triumph.

"All right, I was lying about the brains and stuff," she

admitted. "But I've really been through the door with the light on, honestly."

"What happened?" asked Peter.

"It changed my memory," Amanda said. "I couldn't remember anything that had happened that day, except for a very enjoyable trip to The Vale of Strange."

"So you've been to The Vale of Strange?" asked Peter. "That's more than my Uncle Bob has."

"No," said Amanda. "No one from round here has been to The Vale of Strange. You'd have to be mad to go!"

"But..."

"I said I *remembered* going," Amanda explained. "I never said I'd actually *been*, did I?"

Peter was feeling very, very puzzled. "But..."

Amanda gave a sigh.

"Now pay attention," she said. "If the light above the door is on, The Sweeper's in operation. If you go through, it sweeps your brain. That's why they call it The Sweeper."

Peter remembered what Uncle Bob had told him: "you wouldn't want to be Swept – not like the tourists are."

"So, The Sweeper is for the tourists, is it?" asked Peter.

"You really catch on fast, don't you?" Amanda replied,

then hurried on before Peter had a chance to get angry. "They put it on when the tourists come back from the vale. When they come through the door, they forget what's really happened that day and remember instead an implanted trip to the vale."

"How do you mean, *implanted*?"

"The memory comes from The Sweeper," Amanda explained. "It's beamed into their heads. No matter what happens on their trip to the vale, they always remember a wonderful time. That's why none of the tourists ever complain."

"Even when one of them's died?"

"That's right," said Amanda brightly. "It's always the same happy memory, all official and government-stamped and stuff."

"But when they get home, don't they notice?"

"That one of them isn't there? I thought about that myself, but according to my parents, they're told that whoever's missing has been run over by a bus or hit by a cricket ball or something. My dad says there's probably someone in the government somewhere whose job it is to think up imaginary accidents all the time. It sounds rather like fun, really, doesn't it? I wonder if people ever get hit on the head by falling sheep or drown in goldfish bowls or–"

"But it's terrible," said Peter. "It's deceitful, It's–"

"It's the way we make our living round here, my parents say," said Amanda. "You live at your uncle and aunt's and eat their food, do you?"

"Yes. So?"

"Then it looks like it's a living for you, too."

"But my uncle and aunt are nothing to do with this," Peter protested. "They just keep a shop and–"

"Right," came the voice of Uncle Bob, "that's got The Sweeper fixed. Guaranteed satisfaction again for the tourists, eh?"

"Thanks, Bob," said Mr. Chubb, as the two of them came into view. "We wouldn't be able to run the hotel without you."

Peter turned back to Amanda and saw what he thought he would see.

She had an 'I told you so' grin all over her face.

11
NEW BOOTS

On the way down the hill in his uncle's cart, Peter was very quiet.

"You have a nice time with Amanda, did you?" asked Uncle Bob, as he pulled on the reins to stop the mules from breaking into a gallop.

"Yes," said Peter sullenly.

"She's a bit wild for a girl, perhaps, but her heart's in the right place."

Peter wasn't really sure that people round there had hearts at all, but he didn't like to say so. After all, his aunt and uncle had taken him in, hadn't they? Where else could he go if he didn't like them?

He tried to smile at Uncle Bob, but judging by the look on his uncle's face, it must have come across as more of a snarl.

"Well, perhaps you'll get to like Amanda in time." Apparently, Uncle Bob thought Peter's mood must be down to his new playmate—which, in a sense, it was of course. "We'll buy you some new boots in any case," Uncle Bob continued. "Perhaps that'll cheer you up." But he sounded doubtful.

They carried on down to the foot of the hill and Uncle Bob parked the cart beside a row of shops which was just along from the station. There was a sweet shop and a baker's and a chemist's shop and a post office and a rather tatty shop on the end, with a sign which read, **Boothroyd's Sturdy Boots – heeble-greeb defence a speciality**.

"This is the place," said Uncle Bob, leading the way through a creaky door. "The finest selection of sturdy boots in the country."

The shop had a strong, pungent odour of leather, polish, and cough sweets. A man in a dirty overall looked up from behind the counter.

"Good afternoon, Mr. Arkenthrobb," he said, in a slurpy sort of way, as though his tongue kept tripping over a cough sweet.

"Good afternoon, Mr. Boothroyd," said Uncle Bob. "Got a bad throat again, have you?"

"I've always got a bad throat," said Mr. Boothroyd, "ever since that fizz attack last year. But most of my hair's grown back again, so I shouldn't really complain."

Uncle Bob cast an anxious glance at Peter.

"Ah, yes," said Uncle Bob, "a very *unusual* accident, wasn't it? Now then," he continued swiftly, before Mr. Boothroyd had a chance to argue, "can you provide my nephew here with a pair of sturdy boots?"

Mr. Boothroyd studied Peter with interest.

"Hmm, yes, no doubt," he said. He sucked on his sweet thoughtfully. "What kind of boots is he wearing now? That should be a useful place to start."

"Ah well," said Uncle Bob, looking rather embarrassed, "the lad doesn't actually have any boots at the moment..."

"Doesn't have any *boots*?" cried Mr. Boothroyd, and he made a sort of strangled sound as though he had choked on his sweet.

"Well, not what you call sturdy boots, at any rate..."

"Urgghhh..." said Mr. Boothroyd, clearing his throat. "Doesn't have any sturdy boots? But..."

"He's only just arrived," said Uncle Bob, "and they don't have any heeble-greebs where he came from."

"Ah, I see," wheezed Mr. Boothroyd. "Just got off the train, did he? You were right to bring him straight here. That's why I set up shop so close to the station."

"Well, almost straight here," said Uncle Bob.

"I've only been to Uncle's shop and up to The Strange

Hotel," added Peter helpfully.

Mr. Boothroyd turned a funny colour.

"The Strange Hotel," he cried. "So close to The Vale of Strange? And without any boots to protect him from the heeble-greebs?"

"Well, I told him not to go in the long grass," protested Uncle Bob.

"That's hardly enough–"

"Nor to go standing on thick carpets," Uncle Bob continued.

"Such warnings are scarcely adequate," said Mr. Boothroyd severely. "If you had told him to stand on a chair and stay where he was till he got his boots, that might have been sufficient, but 'long grass' and 'thick carpets'... *Tch*! Heeble-greebs can roll without warning, you know."

Peter wondered exactly what that meant.

"Well, I've brought him now," said Uncle Bob, sounding a bit angry. "So if you could just...?"

But Mr. Boothroyd was staring at Peter's head. "Where's his hat?" he asked, slurping noisily.

"It isn't bogey season," said Uncle Bob. "He doesn't need a hat,"

Mr. Boothroyd gave him a withering look.

"It isn't even July till a week next Tuesday," said

Uncle Bob.

Uncle Bob was turning red in the face now and Peter was starting to wonder if he would get any boots after all. Was Uncle Bob going to storm out of the shop?

Perhaps Mr. Boothroyd's mind was running on similar lines—and after all, he had a business to run. His stern face relaxed into a smile.

"I can lend the lad a hat till you have the chance to take him to the outfitter's shop," he said. "You won't be able to go now because Mr. Limpet has half-day closing today. In the meantime, let's see to these boots, shall we?"

As Mr. Boothroyd emerged from behind the counter, Uncle Bob stood off to one side, quietly grumbling half to himself.

"Ain't no bogeys flying this time of year. Too many folks taking too many precautions..."

Mr. Boothroyd raised an eyebrow and bent to measure Peter's feet. He seemed to be using an odd sort of ruler, a wooden thing with brass buttons and dials.

"If you will allow me to pass a remark, Mr. Arkenthrobb," he said, "I didn't take too many precautions myself last year, now did I? Not when that bogey attacked me."

"Ah, but that was in November," said Uncle Bob,

"right in the middle of bogey season."

"Yes," said Mr. Boothroyd, "but I only stuck my head out the door to see what the weather was like. It wasn't as if I was taking a stroll through The Vale of Strange itself."

"No, but–"

"I'm only saying it's made me realise you can't be too careful" Mr. Boothroyd stood up and squinted at his instrument, tapping one of the brass dials with his fingers. "He seems to be a six and five-eighths," he muttered at last. He went to some shelves, rummaged around, and brought down a big box, from which he produced an enormous pair of boots. "Now then," he said to Peter, "sit down on that stool and we'll get you laced up, shall we?"

The boots were very strong and came up almost to Peter's knees, lacing up at the front. He had never seen boots like this till the day before, but everyone who lived round here seemed to wear such things: Uncle Bob, Mr. Boothroyd, and even Aunt Maggie and Amanda.

"There," said Mr. Boothroyd. "He can go and stand in the long grass now if it takes his fancy. And even walk on a thick carpet," he added in a satirical tone, with a glance at Uncle Bob. Now that the sale was almost complete, he could run the risk of annoying his client again.

But Uncle Bob was in thoughtful mood.

"How much do we owe you for those?" was all he said.

As they made their way back up the hill, Uncle Bob was almost as quiet as Peter himself had been on the way down.

"I'm going to have that talk with you tomorrow, Peter," he said at last. "In the meantime, don't say much to your Aunt Maggie, all right? Don't let on that you don't know much and don't repeat what Mr. Boothroyd said. If you do, it'll get me into trouble."

"So I haven't to say I'm a six and five-eighths?" asked Peter. He turned to look at Uncle Bob but the hat which Mr. Boothroyd had lent him came down below his eyes, so he wasn't able to see very much.

"That's not the bit I'm talking about. I mean the bit about taking more precautions." He stopped the cart outside his shop and turned to look at Peter. "I think we'd better wash that hat and see if it shrinks," he said.

12
Not Enough Tourists

When they entered the shop, Aunt Maggie was screwing the lid on a can of glop.

"That's the last of them," she said. "Enough to kill a whole boggy hollow of bogeys." She placed the can on the counter, next to a great many more.

"What does glop do, exactly?" asked Peter.

His aunt raised her eyebrows and looked at Uncle Bob, who looked a bit uncomfortable. Peter remembered that he'd promised not to let on that Uncle Bob hadn't told him very much about bogeys and stuff. He threw an apologetic glance at his uncle. Oh well—it was too late now.

"Oh, you missed that bit out, did you, Bob?" Aunt Maggie asked in annoyance. "You didn't think it important, then, that our nephew should know what to do with a can of glop?"

"He'll know what to do when the time comes," snapped Uncle Bob.

"He certainly will, because I'm going to tell him now." And she turned her back on Uncle Bob and began to speak to Peter. "You open the can of glop and spread it in a circle around the house," she explained.

"Or in our case, the shop," said Uncle Bob helpfully.

Aunt Maggie turned to glare at him and then turned back to Peter.

"You do this at the start of the bogey season, every September..."

"Every October," said Uncle Bob.

Aunt Maggie pulled a face.

"Every *September*," Aunt Maggie repeated forcefully.

"*Late* September," said Uncle Bob.

"*Early* September," Aunt Maggie said, "just to be on the safe side." And she turned back to glare at Uncle Bob, as though daring him to contradict her again.

Uncle Bob opened his mouth, thought for a moment, then closed it again. "I'm going to get a shower," he muttered, and shuffled quietly away.

"But what does the glop *do*?" asked Peter. "Does it kill the bogeys?"

"It can do," Aunt Maggie replied, watching her husband's departure in satisfaction. "It depends on how much they eat."

"Do you have to feed it to them?" asked Peter.

Aunt Maggie peered at Peter closely through narrowed eyes. "How much did your uncle explain to you about bogeys?"

Peter remembered the promises he had given to Uncle Bob, and all the things like the peculiar clock and the curious can of baked beans which Uncle Bob had promised to show him later.

"Oh, lots," he said, trying to sound convincing.

He wasn't sure Aunt Maggie entirely believed him.

"Well," she said, "no. You don't feed glop to the bogeys. If you ever got that close to them, you'd be dead."

Peter tried not to look too surprised and frightened at this.

"Oh, yes, of course," he said, as though he had known it all along and had just forgotten.

Aunt Maggie gave him a long, probing stare. "The bogeys eat glop of their own accord," she told him. "They very much like the smell of the stuff. That's why they eat it."

"And then they go away and die?" asked Peter hopefully.

"Not usually," said Aunt Maggie. "They don't usually eat enough for that, unless they're very greedy. They usually just eat enough to make them ill. Then they go away again to recover."

"But the glop keeps us safe?" asked Peter, who suddenly wished very much to be reassured.

"Yes, it does," said Aunt Maggie, "as long as we remember to put it down, and as long as we know what glop is in the first place." She threw a hostile glance at the ceiling, from where came the sound of running water. "And we need to remember to take a look at the circle of glop every day," she explained, "because some of it may have been eaten. Any gaps must be replaced and–"

At that moment, a bell sounded and Peter gave a startled jump, his mind running on bogeys. But he saw it was only someone at the door.

"I'd better see who... Oh, it's the tourists!" Aunt Maggie exclaimed. "Well I never...they're bringing back the mules."

Peter saw the man and woman who had eaten lunch at The Strange Hotel standing outside the door of the shop. He dived down behind the counter, afraid that their son might see him. He didn't want to run the risk of being identified as having been up to mischief at the hotel. He had washed away the soot from his face, but you couldn't be too careful, as Aunt Maggie would no doubt say about putting out glop for bogeys.

"There's your deposit back," Aunt Maggie was telling

the tourists. "Did you enjoy it up at The Vale of Strange?"

"Yes," said the tourists cheerfully. "We had a wonderful time,"

"I knew you would," said Aunt Maggie. "The tourists always say that."

Peter realised this would be all too true.

"They brought back two of the mules they hired," said Aunt Maggie, shaking her head as she came back in the shop, "so I had to return their 50p deposits. *Tch*! That doesn't very often happen. We hire out mules to the tourists so they can ride up the hill to The Strange Hotel. Some of them set off walking, you see, but they get too tired when they get this far up the hill. Once they've been through The Sweeper, though, they usually forget to bring the mules back... Where have you got to, Peter?"

Peter poked his head out from under the counter. "Have the tourists gone?"

"Yes," said Aunt Maggie, looking a bit bemused, "but you don't have to hide from the tourists, you know. They aren't dangerous, not like the bogeys are. Has your Uncle Bob been confusing you or something?"

"No," said Peter, coming out from behind the counter. "Er, I was just looking around..."

"Speaking of your Uncle Bob, I'd better give him a shout," said Aunt Maggie. "He'll need to go and round up that other mule. At least I didn't have to return the deposit on all three, which I would have done if they'd all come back. I suppose it's lucky one of them never returned."

Peter's fear of being seen was suddenly all forgotten.

"What did you say, Aunt?" he asked. "One of them never returned? One of the mules, you mean?"

"Yes, and the tourist who was riding it. Only two of the mules returned and only two of the tourists." She shook her head sadly. "It happens, I'm afraid...but at least it's saved us the 50p deposit."

Greatly alarmed, Peter ran out of the shop and down the hill, chasing after the tourists. And then he saw them ahead: the man and the woman descending the hill but with no sign of the little freckled lad. Peter knew the likelihood was that Algernon had been killed by the fierce creatures, yet his parents were chatting happily as they walked along. They would both have been through the Sweeper, Peter realised, so as far as their memory told them, they would both have had a wonderful time at The Vale of Strange.

Peter stopped and stared but couldn't think of any way to explain to them what had happened. He turned round, feeling sick to his stomach, and slowly trudged back up the hill.

13

A Family Meal

"Where were you off to in such a hurry?" asked Aunt Maggie, when Peter returned to the shop. "If you want to burn off some energy, you can help your uncle round up the other mule. It's probably up at The Strange Hotel. That's where we usually find them."

But Peter didn't feel like rounding up mules.

"What's the matter?" asked Aunt Maggie. "You look as if you've seen a ghost."

Uncle Bob came into the shop, drying his hair with a towel. "You haven't been upsetting the lad, have you Maggie?"

Even later, when teatime came, Peter found he wasn't very hungry. He had spent the last hour on his bed, staring into space, thinking about what might have happened to Algernon.

"Don't you like sausage and chips?" asked Aunt Maggie, when she noticed that Peter's sausage and chips were all still there on his plate after five minutes. "Would you like me to make you a sandwich instead?"

Peter shook his head.

"You should have come with me to round up the mule," said Uncle Bob. "That would have worked you up an appetite all right. It ran me a merry chase round the hotel grounds, I can tell you—three times round the crazy golf and twice around the gazebo." He shook his head and helped himself to some more tomato sauce.

Aunt Maggie was looking at Peter thoughtfully. Peter noticed and speared a chip and put it in his mouth. He tried to chew but it seemed to taste like grit. If his aunt and uncle required him to eat, they were going to be disappointed. He put down his fork and pushed away the plate.

"Now then, Peter," said Aunt Maggie, "we have to talk about this."

"What do you mean?" asked Peter, who knew very well.

"We can't have you not eating," said Aunt Maggie.

"Aunt Maggie's right – you're a growing boy," said Uncle Bob.

But Algernon won't be able to grow anymore, will he? thought Peter. *Not now he's dead, he won't.*

"I don't suppose it'll kill me," said Peter, staring down at the table. *But if I was a tourist,* he thought to himself, *you wouldn't even care!"*

"You haven't been scaring him, have you, Bob?" asked Aunt Maggie. "You haven't been telling him more than he needs to know?"

Uncle Bob almost choked on his sausage. "I haven't... *gurgghhh*...I haven't *what*?"

"You heard what I said," said Aunt Maggie.

"I heard what you said but I couldn't quite believe it," said Uncle Bob. "You're the one that's been wanting to tell him more than he needs to know."

"Well, it seems like *something's* scared him enough to put him off his food, and it isn't me that's done it. All I told him was how to use glop. That isn't scary, is it?"

"It depends how you told him about it."

"How do you mean?" asked Maggie.

"Well," said Uncle Bob, "you might have placed the emphasis on the bogey instead of the glop. That might have scared the lad. You might have told him far too much about bogey teeth and bogey claws and the way that bogey eyes seem to follow you round the room. You might have described their eerie cries, and the way it gets cold when they're close at hand, and the way they hover outside your window, peering in with greedy eyes. Then you might have told him about the way they send their victims slowly mad, making horrible scraping sounds that set their teeth on edge, pushing against them with greasy fur and ponging of rotting cabbage. And then it might have got *really* bad. You might have started to tell him about the fizz–"

"I never told him any of that," said Aunt Maggie.

"Oh, well that's all right then," said Uncle Bob, taking a tentative bite of his last sausage.

"But what have *you* told him?" asked Aunt Maggie.

"Nothing frightening. Nothing like that at all."

"How can you be so sure?"

"I just am, that's all."

"I don't see *how* you can be so sure."

"Very easy," said Uncle Bob.

"How?" asked Aunt Maggie.

"Because I haven't told him anything," said Uncle Bob, "all right? Not a single thing. So I can't have told him anything frightening, now can I?"

He spoke with a smug smile on his face, as though he believed the argument was won. But then, slowly, as he looked at his wife, his smile faded away.

"You haven't told him anything?" cried Aunt Maggie. "What do you mean, you haven't told him *anything*?"

"Because I haven't," said Uncle Bob, turning all defensive. "Well, hardly anything anyway. There wasn't enough time."

"Then why did you tell me you had?" cried Aunt Maggie.

Uncle Bob's eyes wandered around the room, as though seeking a possible route of escape. Peter expected he was wondering how things had turned against him. It had seemed to be going so well a moment or two before. His lips moved as he thought to himself, trying to work it out. Then there came a crafty look in his eyes.

"Well, Maggie," he said at last, "when I said I didn't tell him *anything*, I meant to say that I didn't tell him anything *frightening*, you see. This has been a terrible misunderstanding."

"That's where you're right," said Aunt Maggie. "It *has* been a misunderstanding. I used to think you had a brain in your head."

"Now Maggie, that was uncalled for." Uncle Bob glanced at Peter, looking quite embarrassed. "I don't think you're setting a very good example."

Peter made the sound before he realised, so it was just as unexpected for him as it was for his aunt and uncle, who peered at him in surprise.

"Do you have indigestion?" asked Aunt Maggie, for that was the sort of sound it had been.

It would have been easy to say "yes", but Peter had made up his mind to be honest.

"No," he said, "I haven't got indigestion. I made that sound because of what you said, Uncle Bob."

"Oh. I see." His uncle didn't sound very pleased.

"About setting a good example," said Peter.

"Well?" said Uncle Bob.

"What about it?" asked Aunt Maggie.

Peter took a very deep breath.

"I don't think you're setting a good example at all," he said very quietly. "Nobody here at Peculiar Hill is setting a good example. Not for anybody."

For a moment, a sort of stunned silence descended.

"Oh." Uncle Bob finally spoke, sounding all superior. "And what is *that* supposed to mean?" Unfortunately, the effect was spoiled by a rumbling noise in his stomach. "Pardon me," he added.

"The way you let all those tourists die, like that little boy today," said Peter. "I saw him earlier eating lunch, and now he's *dead*." To his surprise, he found there were tears in his eyes.

His uncle and aunt exchanged embarrassed glances.

Uncle Bob cleared his throat. "Ah, yes, well..."

"And his parents don't even know he's dead," Peter protested. "They think they've had a *wonderful* time at The Vale of Strange. But when they get home, they'll be told he's been hit by a meteorite or something."

"Who told you all this?" asked Aunt Maggie. "Was it that girl, Amanda?"

Peter said nothing. He didn't want to get Amanda into trouble.

Aunt Maggie looked at Uncle Bob reproachfully. "I told you that girl would be a bad influence."

"But there's no other kids around here." Uncle Bob protested. "It isn't fair for Peter not to have other children to play with."

"And it isn't fair for that tourist boy to die," said Peter quietly.

His uncle and aunt looked at each other unhappily.

"You say you saw him at lunch?" Aunt Maggie asked.

"Yes," Peter replied.

"How was that?" said Aunt Maggie. "It isn't a good idea to mix with tourists."

"Why not?" Peter asked. "In case they find out?"

"No," Aunt Maggie replied briskly. "It just isn't a good idea."

"Was it Amanda that took you to him?" asked Uncle Bob.

Peter didn't reply.

"And was it Amanda that told you about the meteorite?"

"What?" asked Peter.

"I mean, was it Amanda who told you about the sort of things the tourists would be told?" said Uncle Bob.

Peter kept quiet again.

Aunt Maggie glanced across to her husband. "It must have been. You see?"

"But you're the one who's saying he should be told things."

"Told things in a proper way, not by that wild little girl. Told things by *you*, like you were supposed to."

Uncle Bob looked abashed. "I ran out of time, that's all. I'll tell him tomorrow."

"Tell him now," said Aunt Maggie.

Uncle Bob shook his head. "It's too late in the day. We don't want to give him nightmares."

Aunt Maggie started to speak but then she looked at Peter and her expression softened.

"I'm sorry you're sad but it goes to show that it isn't good to mix with the tourists," she said. "That Amanda should never have let you meet them."

"I never mentioned Amanda," said Peter.

"You didn't have to," said Aunt Maggie. "The way you didn't mention her said everything."

Uncle Bob looked a bit confused. "Er, yes, like your aunt was saying, it doesn't do to mix. It doesn't seem so bad if you don't get to meet 'em."

"But *you* get to meet them," Peter protested. "You hire them out mules."

"Ah, that's different. That's business," said Uncle Bob. "You don't get attached in the same way."

"But if people die, then what's the difference?" asked Peter. "Whether you know them or not, they're still dead. What you're saying–"

But then he stopped. His uncle had held up a hand.

"What was that?" asked Uncle Bob.

They listened carefully and then it came again: a strange creaking sound from out in the hall.

The hairs on the back of Peter's neck all stood up on end. He wondered if it was the ghost of the boy with freckles, come back to take revenge on them all for letting him go to his death. But then he realised he was being silly. It was surely far more likely to be a bogey.

"No," said his aunt, when Peter asked. "I don't see how it can be a bogey. All the doors and windows are locked, and they can't usually chew through the walls." Even so, she looked extremely scared. Strange noises had to be taken seriously on Peculiar Hill.

"Ah," said Uncle Bob, looking rather guilty.

"What do you mean, *Ah*?" asked Aunt Maggie.

"I might not have locked the door of the shop when I came in after rounding up the mule. I was going to get it its feed, you see, but then you started talking and I forgot."

"Oh, I see—it's my fault, is it?" said Aunt Maggie crossly.

"That isn't what I was saying," said Uncle Bob. "I–"

Then the creaking noise came again, more loudly this time.

"You'd better get the pole," said Aunt Maggie fearfully, "and we'd all better put on our hats."

"It's probably nothing," said Uncle Bob. "It isn't bogey season."

"Then what is it creaking?" Aunt Maggie asked in angry panic.

"I don't rightly know." Uncle Bob scratched his head in confusion. "It can't be a heeble-greeb. It wouldn't be able to get up over the doorstep. But whatever it is, I'll soon find out," and he went across to a cupboard. "A bogey pole is very useful, Peter, but if you meet a bogey indoors, you're better with one of these." He brought out a large club studded with nails. "This is a blosh," he said. "One well-placed swipe with this, and your bogey's a goner."

"Now don't you go encouraging the lad to be violent," said Aunt Maggie. "Improper use of a blosh is a hanging offence. Staying indoors with a hat on your head is safest, I always say. Have you got yours handy, Peter?"

Peter said he thought he had left it upstairs.

Aunt Maggie gave a wail.

"You must always keep your hat with you at all times!" she cried. "You'd better have mine for now." And she passed him an orange, broad-brimmed hat, decorated with fruit. "Put it on at once," she said. "Nobody's looking."

Uncle Bob was advancing towards the door.

"And what about *your* hat, Bob?" cried Aunt Maggie. "Don't go out in the hall without your hat."

Uncle Bob shook his head.

"I don't need a hat," he said, "not when I've got my blosh."

Aunt Maggie gave a wail again.

"He's going to die," she cried.

"But what about *your* hat, Aunt?" Peter asked from under the fruit. "You need a hat too."

Aunt Maggie gave a gasp.

"I'd clean forgotten!" she cried, then reached out for a serviette and knotted it at the corners.

"Everyone be quiet!" said Uncle Bob. And he opened the door to the hall.

14
OUT IN THE HALL

Uncle Bob went through to the hall and Aunt Maggie grabbed hold of Peter's arm.

"Don't worry," she told him in a panic–stricken whisper, "he probably won't die." But her body was shaking in so much terror, the serviette dropped off her head. She gave a loud cry of alarm as she bent to pick it up.

"I thought I told you to keep quiet!" came the voice of Uncle Bob.

"Are you still alive?" called Aunt Maggie.

"Of course I am," said Uncle Bob, "but it's very cold out here."

"I knew it," Aunt Maggie whispered in Peter's direction. "It must be a bogey. It always gets cold when bogeys are close."

"It's probably just the draught from the door," called

Uncle Bob.

"Then shut it," called Aunt Maggie, suddenly angry. "He shouldn't have left it open to start with," she whispered to Peter.

"If I shut the door, I might trap the bogey in with us," protested Uncle Bob.

"Then leave it open," called Aunt Maggie. "I have to tell him everything," she whispered.

"Hello, what's this?" cried Uncle Bob.

Aunt Maggie shook her head in annoyance. "How do you expect me to see from the next room?"

"The bookcase is open," said Uncle Bob.

Aunt Maggie raised her eyes to the ceiling. "What is that supposed to mean?"

"The door to my study," said Uncle Bob, "the secret door – it's open!"

"Ah," said Aunt Maggie.

"How can that have happened?" called Uncle Bob.

"Perhaps the bogey opened it," Peter suggested.

"Don't be silly," said Aunt Maggie. "Bogeys can't open doors,"

"Then how *can* it have happened?"

Aunt Maggie cleared her throat. "I think I might have left it open myself," she croaked.

There was a terrible sound from out in the hall and

Peter felt all the blood drain out of his face.

"It *is* a bogey!" he cried.

"No," said his aunt, "don't worry! It's only your uncle losing his temper. He doesn't like me leaving open his study door like that."

Uncle Bob stormed back into the dining room.

"What did you do that for?" he cried, his face all red with fury.

"I forgot to close it," said Aunt Maggie, "just the same as you forgot to close the door to the shop."

"Ah yes." Uncle Bob lost some of his bluster. "Ah, yes, well..."

"Hadn't you better go and see to the bogey?" asked Aunt Maggie.

"Oh, I don't suppose there's a bogey," said Uncle Bob. "The creaking was probably a through draught with both the doors left open." His face relaxed for a moment but then it tightened again in anger. "What were you doing up in my study anyway? You must have been poking about in there to have left open the door!"

"Don't worry," said Aunt Maggie as she folded her arms. "I haven't touched your precious strange tomatoes. I only–"

Uncle Bob gave a cry of alarm and dashed out of the room.

"My strange tomatoes!" he cried as he went. "My strange tomatoes!"

"Uncle Bob takes pride in his strange tomatoes," said Aunt Maggie.

"I know," said Peter. "He showed me."

"Ah," said his aunt, "so that's why he didn't have time to tell you anything useful."

Peter felt bad for a moment or two that he might have got his uncle into trouble. But then he remembered Algernon and he no longer cared very much.

"I suppose we'd better go and check he's all right," said Aunt Maggie. "If his strange tomatoes are damaged at all, he'll need a cup of sweet tea to bring him round."

"Are you sure it's safe?" Peter asked. "Are you sure there isn't a bogey?"

Aunt Maggie sat and thought for a moment.

"Just in case, we'll leave our hats on," she said.

15
THE PACKAGE

When Aunt Maggie and Peter climbed up to the study, Uncle Bob was counting his strange tomatoes.

"Fifty-one, fifty-two..."

"How many tomatoes are there, Aunt?" whispered Peter.

"I wouldn't know," she answered. "He never lets me near them."

"With good reason," said Uncle Bob. "Sixty-four, sixty-five... What a relief. They all seem to be here and safe and sound." He closed the cupboard door. "No thanks to you," he added, glaring at Aunt Maggie. "With the door left wide open like that, somebody could have come in here and taken the lot—like Mr. Grimble, for instance."

"Mr. Grimble wouldn't steal your tomatoes," said Aunt Maggie.

"Oh, wouldn't he?" said Uncle Bob. "I could tell you a

thing or two about Mr. Grimble."

"He's a very good customer of ours, is Mr. Grimble," said Aunt Maggie. "He always comes to us for his liquorice all-sorts."

"Ha!" cried Uncle Bob. "Good customer, eh? Don't be fooled by that. He only comes for a snoop around and to find out what he can about my tomatoes. That man wants his peculiar carrots to win all the prizes at Strange Show. He'll stop at nothing to sabotage my tomatoes."

Aunt Maggie shook her head in exasperation. "Mr. Grimble wouldn't hurt a fly."

"Perhaps not," said Uncle Bob, "but I'm more concerned about what he'd do to a vegetable."

Aunt Maggie pursed her lips. "What do you think that poor little man's going to do? Creep up here with a big axe and set about your tomatoes? Or might he just bring a knife and fork?"

"I wouldn't put it past him," said Uncle Bob. "And knowing him, he'd probably bring some pepper and salt and all, and wash it all down with a glass of wine when he's finished."

"And when's he going to do this? While I'm turning my back to fetch him down the all-sorts?"

Uncle Bob gave a knowing look. "It's funny, you know. There you are on the look-out for bogeys fifty-two weeks a year, not setting foot outside the house except on a Thursday just in case, yet all the time you're entirely blind to the menace of Mr. Grimble, who represents a much more serious threat."

"What?" cried Aunt Maggie. "You think Mr. Grimble's a bigger threat than the bogeys?"

"In the middle of summer, yes," said Uncle Bob, "with all the bogeys hibernating and Strange Show only weeks away. That man has dangerous ambitions for his carrots."

"You're talking rubbish," said Aunt Maggie.

"Oh, talking rubbish, am I? Don't you realise a man like me, who expects big things of his strange tomatoes, is very vulnerable living here at the shop, with all sorts of people coming and going all day long? Any one of them could be up those stairs and doing unthinkable things to my tomatoes before either of us has time to so much as hiccup. That's why I have to keep this study a secret. That's why I have to hide it behind a bookcase the way I do. But then you go and leave it open for hours on end while I'm out so that Mr. Grimble or anyone else could have found it!"

"But it didn't happen, did it?" said Aunt Maggie. "No one's been in here. Not Mr. Grimble or anyone else. Well, nobody else apart from the postman, that is."

Uncle Bob seemed to leap a foot in the air.

"*The postman?*" he cried. "The *postman's* been in here?" He opened the door to the cupboard and checked the tomatoes again—just in case they'd really been missing before and he hadn't noticed. Then he closed the cupboard again and glared at Aunt Maggie. "Why did you let the postman up here?" he demanded.

"He brought a big package," said Aunt Maggie. "I didn't know where else to tell him to put it. That's when I opened the door and forgot to close it again."

Uncle Bob looked around in confusion. Then he saw a large box on the study floor and his eyes bulged wide with delight.

"Oh, it's come!" he cried. "Why didn't you tell me?"

"I forgot about it," said Aunt Maggie. "I was busy making glop. Some of us have to work, you know. We can't all spend all our time on expensive hobbies like strange tomatoes."

But Uncle Bob did not appear to have heard her. He was busy unwrapping the package, scattering bits of paper and twine all around in his eagerness to undo it. And when they had all been torn away, he was left with a long tube.

"Here it is at last," he said, "my guided paintball bazooka!"

16
BAZOOKA PRACTICE

"**N**ow then, Peter," said Uncle Bob, "lob it high in the air!"

Peter hurled the football as hard as he could. A moment later, his uncle fired the bazooka. Its paintball projectile seemed to be aimed too far to one side to hit its target, but just at the last moment, it changed direction and struck the football dead in its centre, knocking it down to land in a clump of bushes. Peter ran to fetch it and found it covered in pink paint. He leant across and pulled it from the hydrangea.

Uncle Bob could scarcely control his glee.

"It works!" he cried. "Just like they said in the catalogue: 'the cutting edge of toy bazooka technology—electronically guided to hit a moving target—not to be used indoors'."

"Can I have a go?" asked Peter eagerly.

When Uncle Bob had invited him to help test the bazooka out in the garden, Peter had not been very enthusiastic. Now that Algernon was dead, it somehow seemed wrong to enjoy himself. Yet the sight of the paintball striking home had driven such thoughts away. To miss the opportunity to splatter something with paint was out of the question. He took the bazooka eagerly and held the sight against his eye, waiting for Uncle Bob to throw the ball.

Afterwards, he swore it had been an accident. Even in his heart of hearts, he was *almost* sure. The bazooka was rather heavy and as Uncle Bob released the ball, Peter got very excited. That must have been the reason why he let the bazooka slip as he pulled the trigger, so that when it fired, the paintball headed not for the ball at all but for Uncle Bob.

Even then, argued Peter, if Uncle Bob had kept his cool and stayed where he was, it might have turned out all right. The paintball would have missed him by a whisker. But when he saw the paintball coming, he tried to get out of the way, so activating 'the cutting edge of toy bazooka technology' which locked it onto its target. In spite of him having the presence of mind to trip over and fall on his face in the mud, it got him in the end—

which was quite a good way to describe it really, hitting him as it did on the seat of his trousers.

"Sorry, Uncle Bob!" cried Peter, putting down the bazooka and rushing across. "Are you all right?"

Uncle Bob sat up and wiped the mud away from his face.

"It hit me, did it?" he asked, looking rather dazed.

"Yes," said Peter, feeling very embarrassed.

"Good," said Uncle Bob. "As long as it works..."

17

NEW AMMUNITION

"Now then," said Uncle Bob, "the reason why I bought the bazooka is to use it as a means of defence against bogeys. I'm not against precautions, you see—it's just that your Aunt Maggie goes too far, not going out except on a Thursday and all. But taking proper precautions at the appropriate time of year is only sensible. That's why I've got the bazooka now, so I've plenty of time to get it ready for when October comes and the bogeys start flying about again."

"Are we going to splatter the bogeys with paint?" asked Peter eagerly, for hitting Uncle Bob just now had only made him more enthusiastic about the bazooka. Truth to tell, he had not been looking forward to seeing his first bogey, but if he could use the bazooka against it, that would be different. All at once, he could hardly wait for October.

But Uncle Bob's response was disappointing.

"No, Peter, that's not what I have in mind. Bogeys are made of stern stuff, and I don't think a little paint's going to scare them away. I want to use some different ammunition...replace the paintballs with something harder, something that will do some serious damage."

Peter looked at the paintballs through the window on the side of the bazooka: all lined up in a row along the tube. Whatever his Uncle Bob said, he wanted to use them against the bogeys. He didn't think firing something else would be half as much fun.

"You've got to remember, this isn't a game," said Uncle Bob, when Peter expressed this opinion. "With bogeys it can be life or death. You heard what happened to Mr. Boothroyd—sore throat and losing his hair and all."

"What exactly *did* happen to Mr. Boothroyd?" asked Peter.

"I'll tell you tomorrow," said Uncle Bob. "It's getting late and I don't want to give you nightmares. Now give me a hand to empty this bazooka..."

Uncle Bob had made a collection of stones he'd found. Each one was about the size of a paintball. He explained that he planned to load these up as ammunition instead, but of course, they made the bazooka heavier than ever.

"It'll take a bit of getting used to." Uncle Bob took the bazooka and did his best to raise it up to his eye. "Get," ... *pant...* "ready," ... *pant...* "with the football, Peter," ... *pant.*

But as Peter prepared to throw the ball, Uncle Bob lost his balance and toppled forwards across the lawn and into the rhododendron.

"Like I was saying," said Uncle Bob, as Peter helped to pick him up and pull the leaves from his hair, "it'll take a bit of getting used to, loaded up with rocks like this, a bit like trying to fire a sack of potatoes."

"Can't we go back to the paintballs?" Peter asked.

"You need to have a bit of perseverance," said Uncle Bob sternly. "You can't go giving up at the first attempt. Now where's the bazooka? (*puff, pant*) I think I'll fire it from over here. Save the trouble of carrying it all the way across the lawn. Lob the football then, Peter, (*pant*). Quickly now!"

Peter threw the football quickly, before his uncle lost his balance again. It flew high up in the air and his uncle pressed the trigger. For a moment, nothing happened, then one of the rocks dropped out of the weapon and fell with a thud to the ground, narrowly missing Uncle Bob's toes. The bazooka made a whirring sound, like a clockwork toy winding down, but the rock made no attempt to follow its target. It lay where it had fallen upon the lawn. A second later, the football bounced about twenty yards away, coming to rest against a garden gnome. The bazooka made a popping sound and Uncle Bob inspected it suspiciously.

"Like I was saying," he muttered, half to himself, "we've got all the time till October to get it right..."

18

Uncle Bob's Little Chat

P eter spent a fretful night. All the excitement of the shooting practice had driven thoughts of Algernon out of his mind, but as soon as he got to bed, they all came back again. Even when he finally slept, the little lad was in Peter's dreams, armed with a bazooka and chasing him through the corridors of The Strange Hotel.

When morning came, Peter felt he had hardly slept at all. He staggered down to breakfast in a daze. There was no sign of his uncle or aunt, but then he heard Aunt Maggie's voice, calling through from the shop.

"Help yourself to breakfast, Peter! Your Uncle Bob'll be down soon. He says you're going to have a little chat."

Something in Aunt Maggie's voice made it very clear

she thought this was not before time.

Peter took a slice of toast and some marmalade, taking care to turn the jar three times widdershins first. From up above, there came the whirr of a drill. It seemed that Uncle Bob was hard at work.

"Just putting an extra lock on the door to the study," he said, when he came downstairs a short while later. "After yesterday night's scare, I thought I'd better conduct a review of security here at the shop."

"But yesterday, the door was open," said Peter. "An extra lock wouldn't have made any difference."

"Very perceptive," said Uncle Bob with a twinkle in his eye. "But from now on, the door will always be closed and locked except when I'm in the study myself. That's because Aunt Maggie won't have a key," He looked extremely pleased with himself. "Now," he said, "shall we have that little chat?"

Up in the study, Uncle Bob brought two stools from under a cluttered table. Both of the seats were covered in grass and dandelions.

"I should have mowed them the other day, but I forgot," said Uncle Bob. "But don't worry—I think you'll find they're comfy enough."

Peter sat down and found that the stool was kind of springy.

"Are these strange stools?" he asked.

"Very perceptive again," said Uncle Bob. "These stools are as strange as they come, except for the one that lights up and makes whooping sounds when you sit down, but that one's broken now. It can't have got enough strangeness, stuck away under that table."

"What do you mean by 'strangeness' exactly?" asked Peter.

"Ah well," said Uncle Bob, "that's what I want to tell you about. The strangeness come up from cracks in the earth's crust, you see. And can you guess where those cracks are?"

Peter thought for a moment.

"In The Vale of Strange?" he asked.

Uncle Bob clapped his hands together.

"Very perceptive again, young man. Very perceptive indeed. And that's why things are so strange in The Vale of Strange."

"So all these bogeys and things...?"

"Are all the effect of the strangeness," said Uncle Bob. "And what you have to understand is that it's just the way it is. There's nothing your Aunt Maggie or I can do about it, you see. Nor the government neither. We don't like it when tourists die but that's the way the world works. It's kind of providing a natural balance, you see."

Peter was losing track of this altogether.

"I don't understand," he said.

"All right, I'll go more slowly," said Uncle Bob. "I'll take it a stage at a time, all right? Everything strange in The Vale of Strange is strange because of the strangeness. You with me so far?"

Peter thought for a moment and then nodded.

"Good," said Uncle Bob. "Now, if things are left to their own devices, they tend to grow and spread, you see—as long as they suit the conditions, that is—and with all the strangeness in the vale, conditions couldn't be better for bogeys and heeble-greebs and stuff. So, if there weren't any humans living here to do something about it, everything round about the vale would slowly get strange as well, and the strangeness would carry on spreading out until *everything* was strange,"

"The whole of the world, you mean?" asked Peter, incredulous.

His uncle wrinkled his brow for a while and then nodded.

"Eventually, I suppose," he said, "but I was thinking more of Peculiarshire—that's what they call it round here, you see, where those of us live who are 'in the know', as we put it."

It was Peter's turn to wrinkle his brow. "Knowing all

this stuff you're explaining, is that what you mean?"

Uncle Bob pressed a finger against his nose in a secretive sort of way.

"Very perceptive again, young Peter," he said.

For a moment, Peter liked this idea of being in the know—it sounded kind of fun—but then he started to feel guilty. It might be fun, but what about the consequences?

"So, all the people who live round here know that the tourists die?" he asked. "Is that what you're trying to tell me?"

Uncle Bob looked uncomfortable.

"Only *some of them* die," he protested.

Peter glared at him.

"Look—I'm trying to make you understand," said Uncle Bob. "Now pay attention, and I'll try and explain why that tourist you met had to die."

This had better be good, thought Peter, leaning forward to listen.

"Like I say, if we humans weren't here, the strangeness would spread and spread. But because we're here, we can keep all the strangeness and weird creatures in check."

"By feeding them tourists?" asked Peter.

Uncle Bob looked startled.

"Er, very perceptive again," he said, "though that's not exactly the way I would have chosen to put it myself."

"But that's what's happening, isn't it? By feeding the strange creatures tourists, we keep the strangeness at bay?"

"Well, sort of," said Uncle Bob. "You are what you eat, you see. So, if the bogeys and other strange creatures eat things that aren't strange, that helps to stop the strangeness spreading out. It's kind of an ecological balance, you see. Like trees providing oxygen for us all."

"Except that the trees can do that without people dying," pointed out Peter.

Uncle Bob looked uncomfortable again.

"Well, as it happens they can," he said, "but that's just the way it is. And the way to stop the strangeness spreading is just the way it is as well. We didn't *choose* to have to invite the tourists,"

"But why don't you feed them vegetables?" asked Peter.

"What—the tourists?" asked Uncle Bob, looking a bit confused. "I think the hotel has a vegetarian option."

"No. The bogeys and things," said Peter. "Feed them ordinary vegetables or other types of creatures instead of feeding them tourists. Wouldn't that work just as well?"

"They've tried all that," said Uncle Bob," and more besides, but nothing limits strangeness like we humans do. Apparently, our PI—Peculiar Index—is minus five, so we're substantially more unstrange than other life forms."

"But it's so unfair to the tourists."

"I'm not going to argue with that," said Uncle Bob, "but it's how things are and there's nothing that you or I or Aunt Maggie or anyone else can do about it."

"But there *must* be some other way!" Peter punched his fists together in anger and then let his hands fall to his sides. He ran his fingertips across the grassy stool.

Perhaps that was it...

"But is strangeness really so bad?" he asked. "You like these strange stools of yours, don't you? And you're fond of your strange tomatoes."

"That's different," said Uncle Bob. "That's strangeness in moderation. Strangeness can be quaint when it's under control."

"But the stranger you make your tomatoes, the better they'll be," Peter protested. "That's what you told me yesterday. The prize at the show will be for the strangest tomato, not the one that's most 'under control'."

Uncle Bob looked at his watch. No doubt he hadn't expected such a long conversation.

"Listen, Peter, the adult world can often be very complex. There's things you might not understand till you're older..."

Peter was getting furious now. He knew that his uncle was being unfair but he couldn't find the words to express what he felt.

"I... I..."

He was turning red in the face.

His uncle didn't seem to know how to respond.

"Er, fancy another bazooka practice?" he asked uncertainly.

Peter ignored him and got to his feet in a rage.

"It's so unfair," he cried. "What's to say it wouldn't be fine if the *whole world* was strange? At least the tourists wouldn't have to die,"

"Look, Peter," said Uncle Bob, "it's only a *few* tourists..."

This remark didn't help at all. Peter's anger was growing. He wanted to do something very bad to Uncle Bob, like smash his bazooka or squash his strange tomatoes.

His eyes fell on the cupboard where the strange tomatoes were kept.

"Now then, Peter," said Bob, hurriedly placing himself between his nephew and the tomatoes, "you're going to be in serious trouble if you don't control your temper."

Something in his tone of voice got through to Peter. He took a deep breath. He had to get a grip on himself and try to think.

"How do things like tomatoes get strange anyway?" he asked. If he kept asking questions, he might find out the answer. And there had to be an answer, didn't there? There had to be an answer which meant that no more tourists would die. There just *had* to be.

"Ah well," said Uncle Bob, pleased to see that Peter was calming down. "The strangeness sort of leaks, you see, so that some of the things that are *near* the vale get strange as well. Like the tomatoes, for instance..." He turned round and seemed to be about to open the cupboard. But then he looked uncertainly at Peter.

"I want to show you something about the tomatoes," he said, "but if I open the cupboard, you won't hurt them, will you?"

One of his eyes gave a funny sort of twitch.

"I won't hurt them," said Peter in a weary sort of way. Uncle Bob appeared to be happy with this.

"Right," he said, and opened the cupboard. But Peter never found out what his uncle had wanted to show him, because Uncle Bob just stood there gaping, his lower lip trembling.

"I... What... But... My tomatoes!" he cried.

Peter came over to stand by his side to see what the matter was. And he stood gaping too. Because the cupboard was just a mass of empty vines. Almost all the strange tomatoes were gone.

19

An Unexpected Visitor

Uncle Bob turned to look at Peter. From the look in his eyes, he seemed to suspect that Peter had somehow managed to take the tomatoes—presumably by magic.

"I didn't do it," Peter protested. "How could I? I didn't have the key."

Uncle Bob glared for a moment, but then his expression softened.

"No," he muttered half to himself, "you couldn't have done it. So who...?"

And then a new understanding dawned in his eyes.

"Mr. Grimble," he cried. "Of course. It must have been Mr. Grimble! He didn't want my strange tomatoes to beat his peculiar carrots at Strange Show." He strode swiftly towards the door, a determined glint in his eyes. From the way he was looking, Peter was glad that *he* wasn't Mr. Grimble.

"I'll get him," cried Uncle Bob as he hurried down the stairs. "I'll see to Mr. Grimble and I'll see to those peculiar carrots of his and all!"

Then Peter heard a door slam and his uncle's voice grew muffled. He went to the head of the secret stairs, trying to hear what was going on.

"No, Bob!" called Aunt Maggie. "Don't take that. Please don't take *the blosh*!"

"I'll take whatever I want," cried Uncle Bob. "Mr. Grimble deserves whatever he gets!"

Some more doors slammed, Aunt Maggie screamed, there were muffled voices, and then there was silence. Peter stood there, straining to hear, but the house felt eerily quiet after all the commotion. Peter wondered what to do and almost went downstairs, but then he remembered that the study was here with its door open beside him. And he thought of all the things that his uncle had told him were waiting inside: the peculiar clock, the wild and wacky sausage machine, and—most intriguing of all perhaps—the very curious can of baked beans. *Why wait any longer?* thought Peter. *It won't do any harm to take a look.*

So, Peter went back in the study, only to find himself

crying out in surprise—for he was looking straight in the eyes of Algernon, the little tourist boy, who was standing there with his hand amongst the few remaining tomatoes, peering back at Peter in abject terror.

20

IN SEARCH
OF DESSERT

J ust for a moment, Peter was terrified too. Was this a ghost he was seeing? Had Algernon come back to haunt them as Peter had feared?

But then Peter saw juice dribbling down the boy's chin, and that was enough to break the spell. He had never heard of ghosts eating tomatoes. He felt a great surge of relief. The tourist hadn't really been killed after all!

Peter smiled but Algernon's eyes were bulging in sheer terror. He tried to lick the juice away, as though hoping that Peter hadn't noticed and wouldn't draw conclusions about the tomatoes.

Peter did his best to reassure the boy.

"Go on, take another tomato," he said. "I don't suppose it'll make any difference now."

But the little boy didn't move. He was still looking at Peter in apprehension.

"I suppose you can't be hungry then," said Peter.

At long last, Algernon's expression began to change. Some of the fear was replaced by concentration.

"Toffee pudding," he said at last, in a small, uncertain voice. "Apple pie, ice cream, chocolate bunnies..." It seemed as though he would go on, his confidence slowly growing, but then he suddenly stopped talking and gaped in terror again. He looked as though he feared he had said too much.

Peter tried to reassure him again.

"Yes, they're nice, aren't they?" he said, peering uncertainly round the study. "But I don't suppose my uncle keeps any puddings up here." *Unless he has some strange ones...* he thought to himself.

Algernon looked so disappointed, Peter was afraid he was going to cry.

Then Peter had an idea. He went to the door and called for Aunt Maggie. As he expected, there wasn't any reply.

The little boy had backed away and was kneeling down to hide behind a pile of strange books. As Peter approached, he heard them whispering, each describing their story, each of them competing to be read.

"It's all right," Peter said. "There's no one else here. My Uncle Bob and Aunt Maggie are out." *Killing someone, probably,* he thought to himself, but he decided it was best not to mention this to Algernon. "Come on," he said gently, holding out a hand.

But the boy looked fearful again.

"Scared," he said. "Bogeys!"

Peter remembered the incident at The Strange Hotel and was glad he' washed his face this morning. Surely he didn't still look like a bogey, not without the soot on his face?

"Ice cream," Peter whispered enticingly, "chocolate cake."

That did the trick. The little lad took his hand and allowed himself to be led across the room. Peter could only hope Aunt Maggie would have such things in her kitchen.

21

ALGERNON'S STORY

"Μy name's Peter. How do you do?"

They were sitting at the dining table, surrounded by sticky desserts. The boy was munching his way through his third helping of chocolate fudge cake and ice cream. Peter very much hoped he wouldn't be sick.

"*Heurgh*," said the boy, shaking Peter's hand.

"What was that again?" asked Peter, hoping his companion might wait till he'd emptied his mouth before he tried to speak again.

"I said hello," said the little lad, having swallowed a large lump of chocolate fudge cake.

"Do you have a name?" asked Peter. Algernon's mother had used the lad's name earlier at the hotel, but Peter couldn't admit that he had been there to hear it.

"Of course I do," said the boy, taking another mouthful of cake.

"Er, what is it?" asked Peter, who decided he ought to choose his words more carefully.

"Aghagha," the boy replied.

"Agatha?" asked Peter, looking surprised.

The little lad swallowed again.

"Algernon," he said. "Any more ice cream?"

Peter went to the freezer and brought him another scoop.

"That's the last," he lied, because he didn't want to be sitting in the kitchen all day. He was worried his uncle and aunt might soon come back. He wondered how long it would take to kill Mr. Grimble.

"I suppose you must have been hungry?" asked Peter, as Algernon quickly ate the last ice cream.

The little lad gave a nod. "I've only eaten tomatoes since yesterday lunch."

"How did you come to be here?" asked Peter. "I was afraid you'd died in The Vale of Strange."

"I haven't been to The Vale of Strange. Too many bogeys."

"You haven't been?" said Peter. "But..."

Algernon's eyes grew wide with terror. "I saw a bogey yesterday at lunch. It was *awful*!"

"Oh really?" said Peter.

"It had enormous horns and pointed fangs."

"No it didn't," Peter protested.

"Yes, it did! *You* wouldn't know. *You* weren't there."

"Oh no, I suppose not," said Peter. In actual fact, he *had* been there, but it wouldn't do to argue.

Algernon looked pleased with himself and took a mouthful of fizzy drink.

"I told my parents I wouldn't go 'cos I'd seen one bogey already and that was enough," Algernon explained. "But then they said they'd *make* me go. That's why I ran off!"

Peter was starting to understand.

"Ah, I see! You ran off. So you never went to The Vale of Strange at all..."

"That's what I said." Algernon spoke slowly, as though Peter were very stupid.

But Peter was piecing it all together.

"So you ran off when you got outside the hotel?" he asked.

"Yes," said the little lad.

"On the way to the vale?"

"Yes," said the lad, looking scared again.

"And you managed to hide from your parents?"

Algernon nodded. "I hid under a bush. I heard them

call but I didn't come out. I didn't want them to make me go to the vale."

"So," said Peter, half to himself, "your parents must have gone back to The Strange Hotel to get some help, but as they went through the door they'd have gone through The Sweeper, so they forgot everything that happened."

"What?" said the little lad.

"So, *they* wouldn't have gone to the vale either, but they *think* they did,"

"I don't know what you're talking about," said Algernon.

"And they won't have remembered you running away, so they'll have gone home and expected to find you there."

"You say my parents have gone home?" Algernon's lower lip began to tremble.

"Yes," said Peter. "I saw them go."

"They've gone without me?" asked Algernon.

"Yes." Peter felt he was being rather cruel but couldn't think what else to say.

Algernon seemed about to cry, but then he brightened and blew some bubbles into his fizzy drink.

"At least they can't make me go and see bogeys now!" he declared happily.

"What happened next?" asked Peter. "After you hid in the bush?"

"I waited there ages but then I looked round for somewhere else less prickly. When I was sure my parents were gone, I ran down the hill, away from the vale. The door was open here, so I came in."

Peter remembered the sound they'd heard yesterday evening while having tea. And the door to the study was left open, so when Uncle Bob went out to look, Algernon must have escaped up there.

"That's right," said Algernon, when Peter asked, "and then I heard voices and hid under all the stuff up there. I came across a very peculiar clock," he added thoughtfully.

So, thought Peter, Algernon must have been hiding in the study the previous evening, while Uncle Bob had checked that his tomatoes were all right. But later, when the door was locked and Peter and Uncle Bob were having bazooka practice...

"There wasn't anything else to eat," Algernon explained, "only those noisy tomatoes. I found a can of baked beans that wobbled and made clucking sounds, but I didn't know how to open it. After I'd eaten, I went to sleep, but you woke me up just now with all your talking." He looked down at his empty plate. "Nice breakfast," he said.

Peter was suddenly feeling guilty. After all, he thought to himself, if he hadn't scared Algernon at The Strange Hotel the previous day, the little lad would not have run off and none of this would have happened. The least he could do now was to try to help.

"I suppose what we'd better do," he said, "is try to get you safely home. Is that what you'd like?"

Algernon thought for a moment.

"My parents won't want to come back again, will they? Back to the vale, I mean?"

"I don't think so," Peter replied. "They think they've seen it already."

"Then it would be nice to go home," said the lad. "I'd like to see my rabbit," he added wistfully.

"I wonder how we can get you there?" said Peter, trying to think.

"I live in Nuneaton," the little lad said helpfully.

"That's nice," said Peter, rather absently. But how were they to get out of Peculiarshire? A sudden noise came from outside and Peter gave a start. Were Uncle Bob and Aunt Maggie back already, he wondered? If they saw Algernon, would they take him back to the vale? After all, Uncle Bob had said that some of the tourists had to die to keep all the strangeness from getting out of control. Would they drag the little lad kicking and screaming off to the bogeys? As Peter thought about this, he gave a shiver. He had to save Algernon – he *had* to!

A noise came again and Peter got very alarmed. And then, as he feared, there came a knock on the door...

"Bogeys!" cried Algernon, hiding under the table.

"No, don't worry! It isn't bogeys," said Peter. And now he had chance to think about it, it couldn't be his aunt and uncle either, could it? After all, they wouldn't have knocked, would they?

"Stay where you are," whispered Peter. "Don't come out until I say. All right?"

"Yes," came the little lad's terrified squeak in reply.

Peter went out into the hall and approached the door.

"Who is it?" he asked. For a moment, he thought it might be bogeys himself. Algernon's fears were getting to him.

"It's me," came a voice which Peter knew. It was Amanda Chubb.

22

AMANDA'S PLAN

Peter tried to think. Was it safe to let Amanda in, he wondered? Would she want to tell her father about the boy? Would he be carried off to the vale after all?

"You can't come in," said Peter, just in case.

"Why not?" asked Amanda.

Peter hadn't expected this. He wondered what to say.

"Everyone's sick," he said.

"Sick with what?" asked Amanda.

"Sick with something very catching," said Peter. "Red spots and yellow lumps and stuff."

Amanda didn't reply for a moment and Peter hoped she had gone. Nothing like an awful illness to scare people away...

But Amanda was still there.

"You say *everyone's* got it?" she asked.

"Yes," said Peter, sticking to his story.

"What do you mean by 'everyone' exactly?"

"Everyone here," said Peter. "Me and Aunt Maggie and Uncle Bob."

"You're lying," said Amanda. "I saw your aunt and uncle only half an hour ago. They didn't look ill at all. Your uncle had his blosh and was in a temper,"

"Ah, that was half an hour ago," said Peter. "They've only just got ill."

He thought he'd done rather well to get out of that one.

"I don't believe you," Amanda cried. "Let me in!"

Peter was starting to sweat now. This wasn't going well. Behind him, he could hear Algernon whimpering under the table.

"I can't let you in," said Peter. "My Uncle Bob has barricaded the door. He's stuck a great plank across it with nails and things,"

"Oh really?" Amanda said, and she tried the door and it opened.

Peter could have kicked himself. He hadn't thought this through...

"Hello," he said, as Amanda stood there grinning.

"Can I come in then?" she asked.

"Help, Bogeys!" came a cry from behind.

"Who's that?" asked Amanda, trying to peer over Peter's shoulder.

"Oh, just a customer," said Peter.

"What do you mean 'a customer'?"

"A customer in the shop."

"The shop's closed," said Amanda. "I came round that way first."

Peter felt very annoyed. This was all going wrong.

"I want my mummy," Algernon cried. "Help! Save me!"

"I recognise that," Amanda said. "It's the little boy from–"

"No, it's not," said Peter.

"What do you mean, 'no, it's not'? How did you know what I was going to say?"

"You were going to say you thought it was the little boy from The Strange Hotel yesterday. But it isn't. So there!" said Peter.

For some reason or other, Amanda looked suspicious.

"I think you're lying again," she said. "I think you've got that little boy in there."

"No I haven't," said Peter.

"I won't tell," said Amanda. "It sounds like a great

idea."

Peter tried to think what she meant.

"What do you mean?" he asked.

"To capture the little boy and keep him prisoner. Shall we tie him up and tickle his feet?"

"You're really not very nice, are you?" said Peter.

Amanda looked offended.

"Don't be horrid!" she said.

"Well," said Peter, "you did suggest..."

"I was only joking," Amanda said. "I wouldn't really be nasty to that boy,"

"Good," said Peter, "I'm glad to hear it."

"But you're a fine one to talk!"

"What do you mean?" asked Peter.

"You're a fine one to come on all goody-goody, aren't you?"

"Well," said Peter, "why shouldn't I?"

Amanda looked exasperated.

"Because you're the one that's holding him prisoner, stupid!"

"I'm *not* holding him prisoner!"

"Yes you are!"

"No I'm not!"

"Help!" Algernon cried from under the table.

"Well it sounds like it," Amanda said.

Peter supposed it did.

"Shall I go away and tell my parents?" Amanda asked.

"You'd better come in," said Peter.

Amanda came in with a broad grin and went to look under the kitchen table.

"Yes, it's him," she said.

"Help! Bogeys!" cried Algernon.

"I think he needs a new pair of glasses," Amanda said.

"It's all right," said Peter. "It's not a bogey. It's only my friend Amanda. It's safe to come out if you like."

Algernon said he would stay where he was, just in case.

"I see you've been having some breakfast," Amanda observed.

"Algernon was hungry," Peter explained. "All he'd had to eat was strange tomatoes."

"That's funny. Your uncle was shouting something about strange tomatoes just now," Amanda remarked. "At least, I think that's what he was on about. It was hard to be sure with his mouth foaming like that."

Peter felt rather sorry for Mr. Grimble.

"So what's the tourist doing here?" asked Amanda. "Or are you going to pretend there's no one hiding under the table?"

Peter thought for a while, then made up his mind he

would just have to trust Amanda. He told her what had happened to the boy.

"Nice one!" said Amanda, when she'd finished laughing. "Pretending to be a bogey like that was a great idea of yours. What a lot of confusion it's caused. Hah hah!"

"Shhh!" said Peter, looking under the table. But Algernon didn't seem to be paying attention to what they were saying. He was too busy peering around for bogeys.

"Don't let on what happened," Peter whispered to Amanda. "It's very important he trusts us. What other hope does he have of staying alive?"

Amanda seemed to be thinking very carefully.

"I see…" she said slowly.

"Because if any of the adults see him, they'll want to take him back to the vale, won't they?" Peter said. "They won't want to let him get away, will they?"

"Er, no," said Amanda. "No, that's right. Especially since he's a child. They're especially keen to see children eaten by bogeys."

Peter's eyes widened in horror. This was worse than he'd thought. "But why?"

"Hasn't your uncle told you? When the creatures eat the tourist children, it keeps more of the strangeness at bay than when they eat the adults. It's because they're fresh and tender you see..."

Peter's stomach lurched. He felt sick.

"But that's horrible," he cried. "You mean to say that when children come, Uncle Bob and your dad...?"

"They don't normally interfere," said Amanda. "They let the bogeys and other creatures take whatever tourists they like, but as this one's been abandoned by its parents–"

"Algernon is a 'he', not an 'it'," said Peter indignantly.

"Oh, whatever," Amanda said, "he or it will be fair game, that's what your uncle will think. He'll probably go and chase the boy with his blosh."

This made Peter feel even worse. He was starting to wish he hadn't had any fudge cake.

"Can I go home now?" Algernon asked from underneath the table. He didn't sound unduly alarmed, so Peter decided he couldn't have heard what Amanda had said. Thank goodness for that! If the boy got scared, things might get out of hand.

"Very soon," Peter assured him, trying to sound relaxed. "We'll set off in a minute." Then he turned back to Amanda. "We have to save him," he whispered insistently. "Will you help?"

For several moments, Amanda seemed to be thinking.

"Umm, perhaps," she said at last. Then she suddenly brightened. "It *will* annoy the adults," she said. "I suppose it could be fun, Yes, all right, I'll do it," she finished cheerfully.

"Good," said Peter. Perhaps she wasn't so bad after all, he thought. And he really needed her help. "What's the best plan, do you think? You know the ropes round here much better than I do. How can we get him out of here without the adults knowing?"

"We'll have to go back up the hill," said Amanda, "cutting through the gully towards the hotel."

"Towards the hotel?" said Peter. "Back up the hill? But surely that's going back towards the vale?"

"Trust me," said Amanda.

"But..."

"You can't do it without me," she said, and Peter knew she was right.

23

A BAZOOKA TOO FAR

They were almost out of the gate before Peter thought about it. Here they were, setting out on a big adventure entirely unarmed. That hadn't happened in any of the movies he'd seen.

"Hold on," he told Amanda. "I'll be back in a moment. You and Algernon hide behind that bush."

He nipped back inside the house and up to his uncle's study. It didn't take him long to find the bazooka. At the end of the practice yesterday evening, they'd replaced the stones with the paintballs again to make it lighter to carry. He strapped it easily onto his back, but then, as he was about to leave, he heard a sound from below.

Oh no...it couldn't be!

But it was.

Uncle Bob and Aunt Maggie were back.

Peter could have kicked himself. A few moments later, he would have been gone. He stood there and listened to what they were saying below.

"I don't know," his aunt was saying, "all this commotion you've made! You'd have terrified the canary, you know. It's lucky it's gone to the vet's to be deloused. And as for Mr. Grimble, it's a good thing it's a Thursday and I could go out. I shudder to think what you might have done if I hadn't been there to hold you back."

"Whatever you say, I reckon we let him off lightly," said Uncle Bob. "Those vases I smashed weren't even very expensive."

"But he says he didn't do it," insisted Aunt Maggie.

"You didn't believe him, did you?" said Uncle Bob. "That man Grimble had guilt all over his face. And you wouldn't let me inspect his teeth neither, would you? I bet there were seeds between them."

"You can't go round assaulting people without proof," said Aunt Maggie crossly. "And you there with that blosh in your hand. You could have gone to jail."

"I only had it to frighten him," Uncle Bob insisted. "I wasn't going to use it. Well, not unless he got difficult, at any rate."

"Well, frighten him you did," said Aunt Maggie. "The poor man was a quivering wreck. He won't come here for his liquorice all-sorts again."

"He only got scared when I threatened his carrots," said Uncle Bob. "See how *he* likes his vegetables interfered with!"

"Where's Peter?" asked Aunt Maggie. "Peter!" she called. "Peter! I bet that child has run away. You were supposed to be looking after him, Bob, instead of dashing out of the house with a blosh in your hand to threaten people with grievous bodily harm. It's your fault if he's run away. Peter!"

Peter thought it best to call and tell them that he was all right—though after what Amanda had told him, he scarcely felt like talking to them at all. To think what they did to children...

"I'm all right!" he shouted. "I'm up here in the study!" He wished now that he hadn't come back. He could have done without the bazooka. He never wanted to see his uncle and aunt ever again.

But then his uncle came up the stairs and Peter did his best to summon a smile.

"I left the blooming study unlocked," said Uncle Bob as he entered. "But you been guarding it for me, have you, Peter? Good lad. Mind you, with most of those tomatoes gone, it's not so important now. There's nothing else much worth stealing," he said, looking around him morosely.

"Er, can we go and practise bazooka?" asked Peter.

"Uh?" said his uncle, looking up. "Bazooka, you say?" For a moment, he seemed to be miles away, but then he seemed to connect with what Peter had said.

"Ah yes, bazooka," he said, brightening slightly. "I had another idea about that this morning. You go on ahead then. I'll follow in a moment. There's a few tomatoes left, I think, so I'd better see if there's anything I can do for them."

Peter gave a broad smile inside. This was just what he wanted: permission to go in the garden with the bazooka. By the time his uncle came out, Peter would be gone.

He descended the stairs quietly, hoping not to alert Aunt Maggie. He heard her through in the shop, opening it up again. Good—the coast was clear! He slipped across the hall and out the door.

"Where on earth have you been?" Amanda asked, waiting where he had left her behind the bush. "Oh, I see, you've brought a toy. You boys and your guns!"

"I don't know what you mean," said Peter. "I'm only being sensible."

"A gun," said Algernon, reaching out. "Gimmee!"

"See what I mean?" Amanda said. "You boys are all the same."

"No, you can't have this, Algernon," Peter told him. "I need to have it...just in case."

Amanda looked exasperated.

"Who are you going to use it on?" she asked. "The idea of this is not to be seen, not to start a war."

"Well, you never know..." Peter said defensively.

"Well, going back for it almost got us seen," Amanda protested. "Your aunt and uncle came back just now. Did you see them?"

"Yes, and they saw me," said Peter, "but I managed to make an excuse."

"And how long is that going to last for?" Amanda asked.

"Er, not very long," said Peter. "We'd better go."

24
UNDER THE HEDGE

manda led the way up the street and soon turned into an alley which ran between picket fences to either side.

"This leads up to the gully," she whispered. "No one'll see us there."

Peter asked what a gully was, but Amanda said he would see in a moment, and led the way as the path turned right between lengths of privet hedge.

Algernon kept asking for the bazooka, so Peter thought it was best to let him hold it to keep him quiet. The trouble was, it was bigger than him and he kept on falling over.

"Can you two get a move on?" demanded Amanda, looking back and noticing that they had dropped some way behind. "We want to get there before it gets dark, you know."

"But it's still only morning," said Peter.

"Even so," Amanda said, as Algernon fell over again. "If Speedy there can't keep on his feet, it'll be night before we know it."

"You'd better give me back the bazooka," Peter told the boy. "Maybe you can carry it when you're older."

"Wanna carry it now!" Algernon wrapped his arms around the weapon as though it were a cuddly toy and accidentally pulled the trigger in the process. As the paintball rose in the air with a *whoosh*, Algernon shrieked and dropped the weapon, running to hide beneath the hedge as though he had been attacked.

"That's right," Amanda said, "keep a low profile."

"Help! Bogeys!" Algernon cried.

Amanda peered each way along the path.

"If anyone comes, we're done for," she said, "but it looks like we might be lucky. We're probably too far away from the houses for anyone to have heard."

"But they might have seen," said Peter, as the paintball fell to the ground with a *splosh*, splattering paint across a clump of weeds.

"All the more reason for us to take more care in the future," Amanda said. "He's *your* little friend, isn't he?

Can't you control him?"

"Come along then, Algernon," said Peter.

"I'm not going. There might be bogeys," said Algernon, squatting under the hedge and looking determined.

Peter looked at Amanda. He was out of ideas.

Amanda lifted her eyes to the sky and marched back down the path to where the little lad was crouching.

"Look here, Speedy," she said, "you get out from under that hedge and take a few steps without falling over and I'll have a quick word with the bogeys and ask them not to eat you just now, all right? Otherwise I'll go and tell them exactly where you are, so they can bring their knives and forks and get you, understand?"

Algernon's eyes grew wide beneath his lenses. He looked like some sort of timid fish, peering out of its bowl.

"Yes," he squeaked. "I understand."

"All right," Amanda said. "Let's get this show on the road then." And she set off up the path again, leaving Peter to coax Algernon out of the hedge.

"It doesn't seem to be broken," said Peter, picking up the bazooka.

Algernon looked at the weapon as though it might bite him.

Peter slung it across his back and took Algernon's hand.

"Come on," he said, "let's follow Amanda. She's not as bad as she sounds, really. She's going to get you home."

25

THE GULLY

B efore very much longer, they reached the gully. It looked a bit like a stream, but without any water.

"That's right," Amanda said, "that's about it exactly. It dried up many years ago. Something to do with the strangeness spreading, they say."

Peter looked uncomfortable.

"Don't worry," Amanda assured him, "you're quite safe out here. It isn't bogey season yet and you've got your boots on, haven't you? That should keep you safe enough from the heeble-greebs."

"Yes," said Peter, "but what about him? Doesn't he need boots as well?" He peered down at Algernon in concern.

"Show him, Speedy," Amanda said. "There you are."

The boy had lifted the legs of his trousers, revealing

a pair of sturdy boots.

"The tourists are all encouraged to buy them when they come to the vale," said Amanda. "Too many toes going missing would be hard to explain."

"You really do care about tourists, don't you?" said Peter sarcastically.

"Look, I didn't make the rules," said Amanda. "It wasn't me who thought of bringing the tourists here. Now, do you want my help or not?"

"Yes, please," said Peter, rather quietly.

"Right," said Amanda, "then follow me." And she led the way up the gully.

"It seems quiet," Peter remarked, holding Algernon's hand as they walked along. "Does nobody much come here?"

"Nobody much at all," said Amanda. "That's why we came this way. I often come down here to play and I never see a soul. People prefer to stick to the road, away from the long grass."

"Because of the heeble-greebs, you mean?" asked Peter, eyeing the ground suspiciously.

"You're starting to get the hang of this," said Amanda.

As they climbed, the gully became increasingly overgrown with weeds and spiky shrubs. Algernon began to protest, and Peter asked if they had much further to go.

"Not much further now," said Amanda. "You see that path over there? That'll take us out of the gully and into the field beyond. Then we'll be very close to the hotel."

She led the way up the slippery path, with Peter and Algernon sliding around behind her. Algernon was growing rather fretful.

"Bazooka?" he asked, holding out his hands.

"You can hold it for a moment," said Peter, as they paused for breath at the top of the track, "but make sure you don't set it off again, all right?"

"You see that fence over there?" said Amanda. "On the other side of that is The Strange Hotel. You two hide beside the fence and I'll go up to my room and get some stuff."

"What kind of stuff?" asked Peter. "No, Algernon— don't touch that. That's the trigger!"

The paintball narrowly missed a nearby cow.

When Peter turned back to Amanda, he found she was already gone, climbing over the fence at the edge of the field.

"You'd better give me that back," he said to Algernon. "I wonder what kind of stuff she means..." he muttered under his breath.

26

SANDWICHES AND SNAKES

"What have you brought?" asked Peter, when Amanda returned.

"Oh, just stuff," she told him, climbing down from the fence. "Stuff we might need, you know." Peter noticed she had a bag slung over her shoulder. It seemed to be quite full.

"What kind of stuff?" he asked, trying to peer inside.

Amanda shook her head in exasperation.

"Things a lot more useful than that bazooka of yours," she said. "You might as well have brought along a big sign saying, 'Here we are, come and get us."

Peter's cheeks burned with embarrassment. "I wasn't to know that Algernon would keep pulling the trigger."

"Never mind," Amanda told him. "No one at the hotel seemed to have seen. My father and mother were out, and—best of all—Bletch was feeding the watch-geese, so even those obnoxious beasts were too busy to notice. And here...I managed to pinch these from the hotel kitchen." She reached into her bag and brought out something wrapped in silver foil. "Sandwiches," she said. "Ham and tomato or cheese and chutney. Tuck in."

Algernon reached out greedy hands and helped himself to a cheese and chutney, while Amanda took a ham and tomato and offered them to Peter. But Peter wasn't hungry.

"Not until we get Algernon safely out of Peculiarshire," he said. "As far as I'm concerned, we can celebrate then. Now where are we supposed to be going exactly?"

Amanda shrugged and pointed along the fence.

"That way is The Vale of Strange," she said, "but the other way," she pointed again, "is a way out of Peculiarshire that not many people use. It's rather steep, you see, and there are snakes."

"But no bogeys?" asked Peter.

"No bogeys," Amanda assured him, tucking into her sandwich.

Peter liked the sound of this. There'd been plenty of snakes on Evil Island and they didn't often bite unless you annoyed them somehow or other, like stepping on them or poking them with a stick.

He decided it might be a good idea to explain this to Algernon.

"If you see any snakes, don't pick them up," he said, but Algernon grinned and carried on eating his sandwich. Peter didn't think he had got through to the little lad. He had a bit of a think, then tried again. "They're like bazookas," he said, "they go off,"

Algernon looked scared and put down his sandwich.

"Don't like cheese and chutney," he said. "Feel sick,"

"You'll feel all right once we get going," Amanda told him. "Come on. Get a move on! We'll stay on this side of the fence until we're out of sight of The Strange Hotel. The watch-geese will probably be sleeping off their lunch, but better safe than sorry." She shouldered her bag and set off along the fence.

"Where are we going?" asked Algernon, as he and Peter followed.

"We're going to take you home," said Peter, "far away from The Vale of Strange forever."

27

THE WATCH-GEESE

Before long, their way was blocked by a hedge which bordered another field. The hedge was prickly and high.

"We can't climb over that," said Amanda. "We'll have to get over the fence instead and out onto the path." She indicated the fence, by the side of which they had been walking. "The trouble is," she continued, "that'll bring us in sight of The Strange Hotel. It'll be quite a long way away, though, so we should be all right. The watch-geese are extremely noisy, but their eyesight isn't the best. I'll go over first and then we'll help Algernon over."

But as she started to climb up, there came a fearful noise in the distance.

"The watch-geese," cried Peter. "They've seen us already!"

"Don't worry," Amanda said, peering over the top of the fence, "it isn't us they've seen. There's a cart driving up to the hotel. It's going very fast. It looks like it might be your Uncle Bob,"

"That would make sense," said Peter. "He and Aunt Maggie must have missed me by now. They'll wonder why I wasn't there for bazooka practice."

"Quickly! Over the fence," said Amanda, climbing over the top of it and dropping down on the other side. "We have to hurry!" she called.

"Won't it be better to stay here and hide till he's gone?" asked Peter.

"No," said Amanda, "go now, while the geese are still making a racket. If they see us now and call out, Bletch won't be alarmed. He'll just think the geese haven't settled down after seeing your Uncle Bob."

"But what about Uncle Bob?" asked Peter. "He might see us as well,"

"He's gone inside the hotel. Now hurry up before he comes out," said Amanda.

She had Peter convinced at last. He gave Algernon a leg up over the fence and then followed himself. A short way away on the other side was a broad path, parallel to the fence, with scrubland beyond. The Strange Hotel could be seen in the distance, its battlements gloomily looming.

"We have to hurry!" Amanda cried, breaking into a run.

"Come on. It's a race!" Peter did his best to encourage the little lad. "The winner gets to hold the bazooka a while." He had a feeling he might later regret this promise.

But the strategy seemed to work. Algernon was running unsteadily after Amanda, and Peter followed on. It was a good thing the path was smooth, or the little lad might have fallen over by now. Peter wondered why the path was so good if nobody came this way? He would ask Amanda later.

A short distance on, Amanda turned to look over her shoulder and then called a halt.

"It's all right. We can rest a moment. We're out of sight of the hotel."

Peter looked back and saw she was right. The hotel had disappeared behind higher ground.

Peter decided to ask about the path.

"It used to be used more," said Amanda, "before all the snakes."

"Why didn't they build a road then?" asked Peter.

"Too steep," said Amanda. "Come on, we've had a rest. We can't stay here all day." And she started out at a sprightly pace, calling back to the others to get a move on.

"I want to hold the bazooka," said Algernon, holding out his hands.

"You didn't win the race," said Peter. "Tough luck—better luck next time, eh?"

Algernon's lower lip began to tremble.

Rather wearily, Peter swung the bazooka off his back.

"Just don't pull the trigger this time," he said. "All right?"

28
THE CALL
OF THE CROWS

W hen Algernon set the bazooka off, it startled a flock of crows. They rose into the air, cawing frantically.

To Peter's surprise, Amanda seemed rather worried.

"Why did you give him that again? Take it off him!" she cried. She peered around her warily. "You might wake something up."

Peter found this hard to understand. She hadn't seemed too concerned before, when Algernon had fired the bazooka where people might have heard, so why should she be so worried out here, in the middle of nowhere?

"What do you mean, 'wake something up'?" he asked.

"I mean what I say," said Amanda, snatching the

bazooka roughly out of Algernon's hands. The little lad looked like he was going to cry. "Don't you start," she told him, wagging a finger.

Algernon looked startled and bit his lip.

"But–" Peter began.

"Maybe we ought to go back," said Amanda. "I shouldn't have brought you here."

"But I don't understand," said Peter. "We're taking Algernon home, aren't we? You said that this was the best way to go,"

"Well," said Amanda, "maybe I was wrong."

"But you seemed so sure."

"Well now I'm not, all right?"

"I don't understand what's changed your mind," said Peter.

"I think it was seeing those crows," said Amanda. "They're a bad omen, you know."

"If you're worried about the snakes…"

"There aren't any snakes," said Amanda.

Now Peter was more puzzled than ever.

"There aren't any snakes?" he said. "But why did you say there were snakes if there aren't any snakes?"

"Because I was making it up," said Amanda.

Peter looked at her strangely. He was getting a very bad feeling.

"I don't understand," he said.

Amanda gave a nervous grin.

"You don't understand a lot," she said. "You're very easy to fool,"

Peter looked at her, trying to work out what it was she was talking about. Then a sudden, awful idea came into his mind.

"Oh no," he cried "You don't mean to say...?"

At that moment, there came a scream, and Peter turned to see that Algernon had wandered some distance away while they'd been talking. He was standing close to the brow of a hill some way further along the path, pointing and crying out in terror.

Peter called out his name and ran towards him, fearing that something awful would happen at any moment. He remembered those words of Amanda's: "*You might wake some*thing *up.*"

"Algernon! Algernon!"

Then, as the brow of the hill drew closer, Peter came to a terrified halt. He could see where the little lad was pointing, out across the valley beyond. It was dark but mottled with tendrils of mist which hung in the air like serpents. Trees and bushes shivered in a breeze which was strangely stale, and something that could not be seen gave a shrill cry of despair.

"It's The Vale of Strange," Algernon cried forlornly.

With a dreadful growing certainty, Peter realised that Algernon was right.

29
AMANDA'S LITTLE JOKE

"Why did you bring us here?" Peter asked in disbelief, turning round and retracing his steps to confront Amanda. "Are you out of your mind or something?"

Amanda looked a bit embarrassed.

"I thought it would be a good joke," she told him with a shrug. "Sometimes I think you don't have a sense of humour."

"A sense of humour?" cried Peter. "But you've brought us here to The Vale of Strange. We might be killed!"

"Look on the bright side," Amanda said. "We probably won't be."

"And all that about another way out of Peculiarshire,

a way that isn't often used—you made all that up, did you? All the time you were leading us here to the vale?"

"Yes," said Amanda defiantly, "and what's so bad about that? I thought it would be fun to see the looks on your faces."

Peter was almost speechless with anger. *Almost.*

"I don't notice you laughing." he said quietly.

"That's because of the crows," said Amanda. "They've made me feel all funny. I think it might be better if we left now." She cast a rather nervous glance at the valley. The tendrils of mist were moving about as though they were alive.

But Peter was far too angry now to be much inclined to follow Amanda's wishes.

"And I think it would be better still if we'd never come here in the first place," he said. "Or if I'd never been foolish enough to trust you. As if you could ever concern yourself with anything else except your stupid jokes."

"That isn't fair!" Amanda protested.

"Oh, isn't it?" said Peter. "And what's going to happen now? Are you going to take Algernon home to your parents, so they can make sure that the bogeys get him? Is that what you're going to do?"

Amanda cast an anxious glance at the little lad. He was standing there with his mouth open, staring down at the vale in disbelief.

"Careful," she said, "you'll scare him."

Peter gave a hollow laugh.

"It's nice to see you're concerned," he said. "You don't want him frightened before your parents kill him, is that what it is?"

Amanda shook her head. "It isn't like that. My parents wouldn't kill him."

"But you said–"

Amanda gave a sigh.

"I say a lot of things," she told him. "Not all of them are true. I thought you might have got the idea by this time."

Peter's head was spinning. He was starting to feel very strongly that he should have been given proper instructions before he came to live on Peculiar Hill.

"Are you trying to tell me–"

"Let's talk about it later," said Amanda. "Right now, let's just get out of here, all right?" She turned and called to the little lad. "Algernon, come on! It's time to go for a walk. Let's go back and have some sticky buns!"

But Algernon didn't respond. He was still standing there in terror, peering out across The Vale of Strange.

"I still can't believe you've brought us here," said Peter. "To put us in so much danger just for a joke!"

Amanda shook her head. "Look, it isn't as dangerous here as you seem to think."

Peter stared at Amanda in disbelief. "I really wish you hadn't said that."

It happened in an instant. One moment, the sky around them was clear except for the tendrils of mist, and the next, something large and black was heading towards them at great speed, something with tiny, yellow eyes and eerie, high-pitched cries. Suddenly, it felt extremely cold, as though someone had opened the door of a house in the deepest depths of winter.

The creature was heading straight for Algernon.

30

ALGERNON TAKES A TRIP

Peter saw with a shock of despair that while he and Amanda had been arguing, Algernon had wandered even further towards the brow of the hill which overlooked the Vale of Strange, as though drawn to the very place which caused him so much terror. Only now did he seem to come out of this spell.

"Help! Bogeys!" He turned to run from the creature hurtling towards him out of the sky, desperately searching for somewhere to hide. Peter ran towards him, calling out his name, though without any idea of how he might save the boy. The distance between them seemed too great now, the creature advancing too swiftly, the sturdy boots weighing heavily on his legs.

"Come back, Peter, you'll never reach him!" he heard

the voice of Amanda behind, yet Peter refused to accept this. He had been trying to rescue the boy but all he'd done was lead him into more deadly danger than ever. He couldn't just stand back and watch this happen.

Perhaps if he could get close enough, he would be able to find a way to fend the monster away. If only the lad wasn't such a clumsy runner.

"Algernon!" he cried again. "Algernon!" But it did nothing to make the boy run any faster, and Peter began to despair of getting close enough to help.

Was there anything else he could do?

He wondered if he should use the bazooka but decided that he had already left it too late. By the time he got it ready to fire, Algernon would have been swept away, and would benefit very little from being covered in pink paint. Instead, Peter increased his pace, straining with every muscle to close the gap between him and the boy. For a moment or two, he thought he was going to make it. He could almost reach out and grab the boy and snatch him away to safety...

But his eyes were playing tricks with him. It was never going to happen. A moment later, with a harrowing, high-pitched cry, the creature pounced upon Algernon, closing its claws on the neck of his shirt and sweeping him into the sky. With a few brisk flaps of its mighty wings, it turned to head back from where it had come, climbing steeply into the sky, far away from Peter's grasping, desperate hands.

"Help! Bogeys!" Algernon cried, as the creature carried him off, struggling like a field mouse in the claws of a mighty owl. Before long, his cries had faded away.

Peter threw himself down on the ground in exhaustion and despair. After all his efforts, he couldn't believe what had happened.

Amanda came to stand beside him.

"At least he knew what got him," she said. "That was a bogey all right."

Peter couldn't say a word. He just lay there and beat the ground with his fists.

"You'd better not lie down there for long. The heeble-greebs will get you," warned Amanda. "Sturdy boots won't help much if you're lying down."

Peter could scarcely control his despair and fury. "I don't care if they get me. I don't deserve to live. Because of me, that little boy's going to die!"

"I think you're being too hard on yourself," said Amanda. "It's more because of me than you, I'd have thought."

Peter sat up and glared at her.

"You're right there," he said. "You led us into this

trap. Is this what you thought would happen all along?"

"Of course not," said Amanda. "The bogeys don't normally fly till November, and it isn't even July till a week on Tuesday."

"I think I've heard that somewhere before," muttered Peter.

"Well then," Amanda replied, "you'll understand why I couldn't have known that would happen. It's really a great shame. But he's only a tourist."

Peter jumped to his feet, full of fury.

"Only a tourist?" he cried. "That's what you people think round here, isn't it? The tourists aren't even real people, as far as you're concerned."

"Well, yes they are," Amanda protested. "It's just that we don't know them. It's not the same as people who live here."

"But it is the same, don't you see?" said Peter. "The tourists are people, the same as us. They don't deserve to die any more than we do."

"It's not about deserving," Amanda argued. "It's more about the way–"

"The way the world works," said Peter wearily. "Yes, I think I've heard that before as well. But I don't believe it has to be like that. I don't think people should have to die, whether we know them or not. There has to be a way for that to change."

Amanda shook her head in disbelief. "You really have some funny ideas."

31
Peter Makes a Decision

"You think we were just unlucky then, do you?" asked Peter. "We were just unlucky to come across a bogey like that?"

"Yes," said Amanda, "we were unlucky. If it hadn't have been for those crows, I'd never have guessed it could happen. And yet, at the same time, you could say we were lucky as well."

Peter could hardly believe what she had said.

"How do you work that out?" he asked. "Lucky not to be all killed, you mean?"

"Lucky the bogey didn't fizz us," she said. "Bogeys often do. And that could have been very nasty indeed, especially as you're not even wearing a hat."

Peter felt the top of his head.

"Oh no, I left it at home." he said. "Mind you," he added, giving Amanda a glare, "I might have brought it along if I'd known we were coming here."

Amanda rummaged about in her bag and produced a hat.

"Here," she said, "you'd better have this, and make sure you put it on. It's silly not to wear a hat with bogeys about."

Peter put the hat on and felt it sort of sag around his head. It was scarcely a better fit than the one at home, but at least this one wasn't covered in fruit like his aunt's had been.

"Anything else I should have?" he asked. "I've got the boots and I've got the hat. Is that enough?"

"That should see you safely home," said Amanda.

"What makes you think I'm going home?" asked Peter.

"Well, where else–" Amanda began, then stopped up short. "Oh no, Peter," she cried, "you can't be meaning to–"

"Go after Algernon?" Peter asked. "Is that what you were going to say? Full marks, Amanda, because that's exactly what I'm going to do."

"Now then, Peter, you have to be sensible."

"Sensible!" cried Peter. "That's rich, coming from you,

Amanda. Since when have you ever done anything sensible?"

"I'm doing it now," said Amanda. "I'm telling you to go and forget about Algernon. I'm sorry myself about what happened. He was kind of sweet, I suppose," she added doubtfully. "But going into The Vale of Strange would be very stupid indeed. You probably won't come back again—and what's the use of killing yourself for nothing?"

"It's not for nothing," Peter insisted. "I'd be going after Algernon. I'd die in a worthy cause. But I don't suppose that's anything you would understand."

"You're not going to get anywhere by insulting me," said Amanda. "I'm still going to tell you not to go, however horrid you tell me I am, because I've lived here longer than you, so I know what's right."

"What's right?" cried Peter. "Let me remind you, you brought us here for a joke. You seem to think the right thing to do is to put all our lives in danger just for your amusement."

Amanda's eyes started to glisten.

"I didn't know I was putting our lives in danger," she insisted. "There aren't usually bogeys about at this time of year. I didn't know Algernon was going to be snatched away like that. I didn't!" She wiped away an angry tear and folded her arms defensively. "And what's the point of anything, if you can't have a bit of fun?" she added sulkily.

"Right then, I'll see you Amanda," said Peter. "Or else not, as the case may be." He turned away and set off towards the vale.

"Look, you're being very stupid, Peter. You don't know what you're getting into," Amanda called after him. "Even if you don't get eaten yourself, how are you going to find a single bogey in all the vale? And how do you even know that Algernon isn't already dead?"

Peter stopped in his tracks. He didn't have the answers to any of this.

"Well," he said, "maybe you can help me."

"Oh no," said Amanda, "you can be a fool if you like, but I'm not going to throw my life away for nothing. All right, all right, I know you're thinking of Algernon, but believe me, that boy is already a lost cause."

Peter couldn't help but suspect she was right. Even so, what was the alternative? He still felt guilty for what had happened, even if Amanda didn't. He couldn't just go home to the shop and pretend that nothing had happened.

"Goodbye, Amanda," he said, and carried on.

"Come back, Peter!" shouted Amanda. "You're really

being very, very stupid. You'll go down there and never come back, and then what am I supposed to tell your aunt and uncle?"

Peter stopped and looked back at her for a moment.

"I've only been here a few days," he said. "Just tell them to think of me as a tourist. That should ease their minds. Then nobody needs to lose any sleep, do they?"

And he carried on towards the dark, brooding valley, where somewhere a certain bogey dwelt in its boggy hollow, and where hopefully Algernon clung onto life, waiting to be saved.

32

THE JAMJAM PLANT

As Peter descended into the vale, the air became heavy and sort of purple, as though it was one part air and one part blackberry jelly. He felt as though he were looking through a purple-tinted mask, which gave the afternoon the feel of twilight.

Underfoot, the ground grew boggy. Peter's boots made sploshing sounds as he walked along, past plants that became gradually taller and more peculiar the farther he went. He was sure that when his eyes were turned, the plants were moving to get a better look at him, peering at him through secret eyes in their strangely formed flowers.

He began to wonder if Amanda hadn't been right. Perhaps he should have accepted the fact that Algernon had been taken, one more tourist lost to The Vale of

Strange. What hope did Peter have of finding the little lad, here in this awful, purple place he had never been before, where even the plants seemed to resent his presence?

Not for the first time, he stopped and listened, thinking he'd heard a noise behind him. But as he peered over his shoulder, all he could see were the plants he'd passed a moment before, their leaves and feelers moving in the breeze. Although, now that he thought about it, there didn't seem to *be* any breeze. He couldn't feel anything cold against his face.

Perhaps the plants were moving because he'd brushed them as he passed? Or perhaps he was right and the plants really were moving to get a look at him. Or perhaps they were moving because–

Peter didn't have time to complete this thought. The feelers shot out from one of the plants as though they'd been fired from a gun and wrapped around his legs. They seemed to deliberately lift him up, so he lost his balance and footing, and crashed down onto his back. The feelers moved swiftly, now, wrapping themselves round every part of his body, wriggling across him like hairy worms and pinning his arms and legs so he couldn't move. Then as he lay there, staring up at the heavy, purple sky, vaguely aware of the tendrils of mist above, he felt something cold and runny oozing across his body, as though he were being coated in sticky jam.

At first, he thought the bazooka must have been smashed in the fall and its paintballs splosed across him, but craning his neck and pulling against the hairy feelers which held him tight, he could just make out the bazooka, lying unbroken where it had fallen beside him. He considered trying to reach it, but he knew the feelers were too strong. Even if he managed to get it, what good would it do? It wouldn't help to cover the feelers in paint.

And then, as he lay there, something clouded his vision and stung his eyes, and he realised that whatever had oozed across his body was now all over his face as well. He could feel it dripping down into his mouth. It tasted like fiery curry sauce and under-ripened apples. Peter wasn't at all fond of curry.

"I can't leave you for five minutes, can I?"

For a moment, Peter thought he was hearing things. He knew that he was entirely alone, and yet...

"Amanda?"

"Who do you think it is, stupid? Your Aunt Maggie?"

"But I thought—"

"You don't seem to think very much at all, it seems to me. Five minutes here in the vale and you're trapped by a jamjam plant. I thought you might have lasted a bit longer."

"I'm all covered in sticky stuff," said Peter, sounding as clearly as might be expected from someone whose mouth was oozing spicy jam.

"Yes, you would be," Amanda said impatiently. "That's how jamjams work. First they trap you with their feelers and then they spout that stuff like strawberry jam. The best way to think of it is like gastric juices, you see. The same stuff we produce ourselves when something reaches our stomach. And that's perhaps the easiest way to think of yourself right now. You're a piece of food in the jamjam's stomach, slowly being digested. All very clever isn't it? For a plant, I mean."

Peter supposed it was, but he wasn't impressed. Something else was on his mind, but he hardly dared mention it to Amanda in case she didn't give him the answer he wanted. Even so, he'd have to give it a try.

"Er, is there anything you can do to help me?" he asked, with a tentative gurgle.

Amanda gave a sigh.

"As it happens, there is," she said, "lucky for you. Otherwise you'd just have to lie there, slowly being digested. It would take a very long time though. The jamjam plant doesn't exactly bolt its food, you see. Even so, in a few months' time, there wouldn't be very much left of you, except that the plant would probably have grown a lot taller."

"You mentioned something about being able to do something," said Peter, anxious to get Amanda back to the nub of the conversation. "What was that, exactly?"

"I'll give you a squirt with this," said Amanda, waving an aerosol can in front of Peter's face. "Close your eyes."

Peter did as she asked and felt a fine spray against his skin. Then he felt the feelers which held him begin to release their grip. Eagerly, he struggled free and managed to get to his feet. It felt so good to be able to move again. He spat out globs of spicy jam and wiped himself with his handkerchief.

He looked down and saw that the ground was covered in some sort of foam. The plant's feelers were shrivelling up, writhing about as though in pain as they did so. The foam which Amanda had squirted seemed to be eating them up as though it were made of acid.

"What *is* that stuff?" asked Peter.

Amanda read from the can.

"It's called 'Mr. Puddle's Unctuous Splodger for the urgent control of jamjams, plarks, spiky gobbles, and other carnivorous plants. Not to be taken internally. Do not squirt in the eyes.' Your Aunt Maggie sells it in her shop."

"I haven't seen it," said Peter.

"It won't be much in demand, I don't suppose," Amanda told him. "The plants are rather clever, but they can't come out of the vale, so nobody needs to worry about them unless they're intending to venture inside, and hardly anyone ever does. Except the tourists, of course."

"And no one's going to tell them they might need it, of course," said Peter sarcastically.

Amanda put the can in her bag and glared at him. "I was hoping you might have changed your attitude after I rescued you like that. Some people might have been grateful."

"Thanks, Amanda," said Peter, feeling slightly abashed.

"That's all right," said Amanda, rather haughtily. "Now might I enquire what you intend to do next?"

"I'm going to look for Algernon," said Peter.

Amanda gave a sigh.

"Haven't you learnt?" she said. "It's dangerous in here. If you go any further in, you'll probably die."

Peter thought for a moment.

"But most of the tourists don't die," he said. "Most of them come back safely. Is it really as dangerous as you say?"

Amanda raised her eyes to the purple sky.

"The tourists don't get very far inside the vale," she said. "As soon as they see someone else attacked, they all run off screaming. That's the only reason so many survive."

"But that can't be right," Peter protested. "Uncle Bob said most of the tourists have a perfectly good time in The Vale of Strange,"

Amanda gave him a look as though he were mad. "That might be what they remember, but only because they've been through The Sweeper, stupid! They don't really have a good time at all."

Now that Peter thought about it, he could see this must be true. He was going to have a few stiff words with Uncle Bob.

"Even so, I have to look for Algernon. I can't just leave him to die," Peter protested.

Amanda shook her head in exasperation.

"And do you by any chance want me to help you?" she asked.

Peter smiled in what he hoped was a charming way. "If you wouldn't mind."

"All right," said Amanda. "But if I die, I hope you'll feel as bad about me as you do about that tourist. Or do you only care about people who keep falling over?"

Peter tried to think about this. He had rather mixed feelings about Amanda. But even so, if it wasn't for her, he'd still be trapped by the plant.

"It was good of you to come after me," he said. "What changed your mind?"

"Nothing changed my mind," she said. "I was always going to come after you. I only said I wouldn't do, to try to persuade you not to be so stupid. But now I've given up. If you insist on being stupid, I don't suppose there's very much I can do about it."

"But you could be clever and go back," said Peter.

"That's right," Amanda agreed, "but I know you won't survive without me, so that's why I'm being stupid as well. People might almost get the idea I liked you, I suppose. Let's get started then, shall we?"

And she brushed past him and led the way further into the vale.

33

THE EXPLODING HOOPLA

After a while, it grew less boggy and overgrown with plants. The narrow path they had followed between the plants broadened, and Peter began to feel a bit less tense. He had been afraid of another attack from a jamjam plant, or perhaps from a plark or a spiky gobble, or one of the other plants mentioned on the can of Mr Puddle's Unctuous Splodger. But now that the towering plants were further away, with closer at hand a cluttered tangle of what appeared to be harmless weeds, he could breathe a bit more easily, even though he was well aware there would be plenty of other dangers lurking in the gloomy Vale of Strange.

And even as he thought about this, he heard a sort of a whoop nearby and saw a dazzling light amongst the weeds. Acting on instinct, he crouched down and got the bazooka ready to fire, calling out to Amanda to take cover.

But she just stood there and laughed.

"What are you doing?" she asked. "Who are you going to shoot?"

"I thought someone was firing at us," said Peter.

"You've seen too many movies," Amanda told him. "That was only a hoopla. Nothing to worry about."

Peter got to his feet again.

"What's a hoopla?" he asked, rather annoyed. Even though it was not his fault, it made him feel stupid to know so little about The Vale of Strange. He felt he should have been taught about it at school on Evil Island, instead of all that useless stuff about coconuts.

"A hoopla's a plant," Amanda explained, "but it isn't dangerous—not like the jamjam plant. Well, not to someone as big as us, at any rate. If something brushes up against it, it goes *whoop* and explodes. A field mouse or a heeble-greeb would probably get roasted, but the worst you or I would get is a scalded foot."

Even so, Peter thought, that wouldn't be very nice.

"What do they look like?" he asked for future reference.

"Come and look," said Amanda, leading the way amongst the weeds. "There's no need to worry too much—you're wearing your sturdy boots. You see over there, where the weeds are scorched? Those bright yellow plants are the hooplas. Probably something small and furry set one off just now. I don't suppose there's very much of it left."

But something else amongst the weeds caught Peter's eye.

"What's over there?" he asked, advancing towards it.

"Careful, Peter," Amanda warned him. "I can't see what you're looking at. Show me."

"Those round, shiny red things," said Peter, pointing them out.

Amanda started laughing again. "Those aren't very dangerous either. Those are tomatoes."

"That's what I thought," said Peter. "But are they strange tomatoes, you think?"

"I expect they will be," Amanda said, "almost everything's strange, here in the vale."

"In that case," said Peter, "have you got any space in that bag of yours?"

"If you're feeling hungry, I've got a few sandwiches left," said Amanda.

"Oh no," Peter replied, "I'm not intending to eat them. They're a present for somebody else." Though I'm not really sure he deserves them, he thought to himself.

34

THE BUBBLING BOULDER

A bit further on, they came to an open space. Peter was getting rather tired and suggested they should stop for a while and have some more sandwiches.

"All right," said Amanda, but when Peter sat on the grass, she shouted a warning. "No, Peter, you can't do that! There might be heeble-greebs about."

Peter jumped up and looked warily round him. Even in the open space, the grass was rather long. He should have known better by now. Would he ever get used to life in Peculiarshire?

"If you lose a finger or two, that'll probably teach you," Amanda told him. "Every time you try to add up to ten, you'll be reminded."

"I can count without using my fingers," Peter protested.

"All the more reason to try to stay alive then," Amanda replied. "It would be a shame to waste all that education."

Amanda was still getting at him. If she hadn't saved his life, he might have got cross.

"Look, we can sit on those," said Amanda, pointing across to a nearby group of boulders. "The heeble-greebs can't climb up them. The rock's too hard for them to get their teeth in."

"What are they like, these heeble-greebs, exactly?" Peter asked.

"You'll find out soon enough, I expect," said Amanda.

"It's just that I've heard them mentioned so much but... *Aaagh*! Hey – what's happening?"

He had been about to climb up on one of the boulders when it suddenly started to bubble like a saucepan of simmering milk. Bits of it kept bulging, then flattening out again.

"Just ignore it," Amanda said. "It's only being strange. It'll probably stop in a moment or two, I expect." She climbed on an adjacent boulder and held a sandwich out to Peter. "Cheese and chutney?"

"Er, thanks." Peter took the sandwich and selected a

different boulder. Lumpy seats were all very well but not if the lumps kept moving about. He didn't want to sit on something that seemed to be alive.

"Don't worry about it," said Amanda. "It's only lumps of strangeness moving about. In a moment, they'll turn into frogs or something and that'll be that."

As Peter watched, the bubbling boulder turned into a large spotted beetle, which slowly crawled away across the grass.

Peter stared at it with his mouth gaping open.

"You should shut your mouth while you're eating," said Amanda.

"Can that happen to anything?" asked Peter.

"What do you mean?" asked Amanda.

"Changing into a beetle like that – could that happen to anything here in the vale?"

Amanda gave a shrug.

"Anything could happen, but it usually doesn't," she said. "That's because the tourists help to keep the strangeness at bay. But imagine how it would be if they didn't come here. There'd be things becoming beetles and stuff all over the place."

Peter took a thoughtful bite of his sandwich. That was all very well, but surely there must be some other way to keep the strangeness at bay. A way that didn't mean people had to die.

Amanda finished her sandwich and started rooting about in her bag. Peter caught sight of something that looked like a toy horn.

"What did you bring that for?" he asked.

"Never you mind," said Amanda. "You'll find out soon enough if we happen to need it."

But Peter was curious what else she'd brought in her bag.

"Just some things that might be useful," Amanda said, when he asked. "Things I've read about in books and other things that have come in useful before when I've been in the vale–" She stopped up short and coloured slightly. "Ah, I wasn't meaning to tell you that."

Peter gaped at her in astonishment. "You've been in the vale before? But I thought–"

"Promise you won't tell anyone?" asked Amanda. "Especially not my parents. I'll get into trouble."

"Of course I won't tell them," Peter said, "but I don't understand. I thought that no one who lives round here ever goes into the vale, because everybody knows it's too dangerous."

"Well," said Amanda, "that's almost right. Except for a few explorers..."

Peter's eyes widened at this. He really liked

explorers. He'd met them before on Evil Island. They used to wrestle crocodiles and stuff like that.

"Explorers?" he said excitedly. "Explorers live round here?"

"Well, not anymore," Amanda said. "They're all dead now, actually. They all went into the vale and never came back."

All of a sudden, Peter felt rather scared. As he watched, some worms emerged from out of a nearby boulder. Overhead, the sky was turning green.

"Didn't it used to be purple up there?" he asked.

"It changes from time to time," said Amanda, matter-of-factly. "You should see it when it's yellow with pink spots. Shall we get on?"

She slid down from her boulder and led the way across the clearing, with Peter hurrying warily behind.

35

THE ATTACK OF THE HEEBLE-GREEBS

"I get so bored," Amanda explained as they walked along. "Like I say, no one from school wants to come so close to the vale. They're scared of all the bogeys and stuff, I suppose. So sometimes I'm stuck there all on my own in The Strange Hotel, and I get so bored, I'll do anything for a laugh."

"So you come to the vale?" Peter asked. "You really do?"

"What's such a big deal? You're in the vale as well, aren't you?"

"But I'm here for a reason. I'm here to rescue Algernon."

"I go in for a reason as well. To take a look around the place. You can't really live so close and not be curious."

"The adults seem to manage it," said Peter. "Apart from the explorers, I mean."

"The adults don't have any imagination," said Amanda. "That's how they can do what they do to the tourists. They don't really think about what's going on. They can't imagine how the tourists must feel."

"And you *can*?" asked Peter in surprise. Amanda hadn't seemed to care about the tourists any more than anyone else did.

"Yes, I can," Amanda replied, "but I usually don't. Because if I did, I'd be too upset. After all, there's nothing I can do about it, is there? I'm only a child. What's the point in getting upset about something you can't change?"

Peter thought about this.

"But it won't be like that always," he said. "There'll come a time when you're old enough to change what's going on. So don't pretend it isn't happening. Otherwise, when you grow up, you might forget to change it after all."

Now Amanda grew thoughtful.

"Yes, you're right..." she began.

Clack-a-clack! Clack!

Peter looked down in alarm to see what appeared to be a bunch of rocks attacking his legs and feet. They were jumping up and down, banging into his boots.

"Heeble-greebs," said Amanda. "I told you we'd come across them before very long. Aren't you glad you're wearing your sturdy boots?"

"I only hope they're high enough," said Peter. The heeble-greebs were jumping as high as the calves of his legs.

"Don't worry. It's all been scientifically tested," said Amanda. "The highest recorded heeble-greeb jump is nine and a quarter inches. You're quite safe as long as you don't sit down."

With the clacking sound of the heeble-greebs' jaws opening and closing against their boots, Amanda's warning was scarcely needed, but Peter bent down a short way to try to get a better look at the creatures.

They were moving so fast, it was very hard to make out much about them. They were brown and round and that was about it.

"Wait a moment. I've got some gloves," said Amanda. "You can pick one up and take a better look."

"P...P...Pick one up?" he stuttered. She had to be joking!

"With a pair of sturdy gloves, I mean." She brought a pair of enormous gauntlets out of her bag and put them on. Then she bent down and picked up one of the heeble-greebs, holding it between finger and thumb to show it to Peter.

Peter was very suspicious at first, but she told him not to worry.

"I'm holding it very firmly," she said. "You can come a little bit closer. There you are. You can see all its mouths and eyes and tentacles now. If you count them, you'll find that there's six of each, spaced equally over its body."

Peter would take her word for it. At any rate, there seemed to be an awful lot of all of them. Even held in Amanda's hand, the heeble-greeb was in constant motion: gnashing its teeth, wriggling its tentacles, and peering at them maliciously with its eyes.

"It uses its teeth for biting," Amanda explained, though this was something which Peter had already worked out for himself. "It bites to eat," she continued, "but also to help it get around. It can bite into soft ground and use the teeth as an anchor, you see. If you didn't have your boots on, it could climb up your legs like that."

Feeling a bit faint and hoping he wouldn't fall over, Peter looked around for a nice, safe boulder on which to climb out of danger, but didn't see one. He understood now why people took these little creatures so seriously.

Amanda continued her impromptu lesson on heeble-greeb anatomy. "It also uses its tentacles to get around. It uses them like flippers to change direction, then rolls along. When it wants to stop, it digs in with its teeth."

Peter found the tentacles particularly unpleasant. They looked like little worms, wriggling their way out of the creature's body.

"The tentacles are also what allow it to jump," said Amanda. "It uses them like springs to give it lift. And it sometimes uses the tentacles to hold its food while it's eating. It can't hold on with its teeth and eat at the same time, you see."

Peter could understand this might be difficult, but he couldn't work up much sympathy for the creature.

"So," said Amanda, "at any one time, you can see about half the heeble-greeb's body, okay? What you can see are three eyes, three mouths, and three tentacles. They all seem to be jumbled up because we're used to looking at two eyes, a nose, and a mouth on a face, and this is a little bit different..."

A little bit different? That wasn't exactly the way Peter would put it himself.

"But they're all spread out evenly," Amanda continued. "You can see if you look closely. And the other three of each are round the other side of its body."

Peter thought he understood, but rather wished he

didn't.

"But all you really need to know is to stay out of their way," said Amanda, "and never pick them up unless you're wearing sturdy gloves. I've brought a pair for you as well, so you can have a go."

Peter wasn't very enthusiastic about this. "Er, maybe we ought to move on and look for Algernon."

Amanda gave a grin.

"You're frightened of them, aren't you?" she asked.

Peter thought for a moment he might pretend, but decided against it.

"Yes," he admitted, "I'm terrified."

Amanda was still grinning.

"Good," she said. "So am I. That's the only way to be. Once the greebs stop scaring you, you're in trouble." She put the creature down again, where it threw itself against her boots, angrily clacking.

"Come on," she said, "you're right. We should get a move on."

"You called them 'greebs' just now," said Peter, as they left the creatures behind. The creatures had pursued them a while but had soon given up. "I've only heard them called 'heeble-greebs' before."

"'Greebs' are what the greeb fanciers call them," Amanda explained. "The men who take them to Strange

Show and enter them in contests and stuff like that."

Peter said that this sounded unlikely.

"People think they're mad," said Amanda, "keeping strange creatures like that—but is it really any more weird than growing strange tomatoes?"

"Not any more weird," said Peter, "but lots more dangerous, surely? How do they carry the things about? In armoured cars?"

"No, just in sturdy bags," said Amanda. "They carry the greebs around with them like bowling balls. It's just another kind of sport, they say. They hold lots of contests with them to see how high they can jump, and fastest through an obstacle course and stuff like that. There's even a prize for depth of bite on a piece of cheese– What's the matter?"

Peter had stopped dead in his tracks and was staring at Amanda.

"What did you say?" he asked.

"I said there's a prize for depth of bite on a piece of cheese," she repeated. "They usually use gorgonzola because–"

"No, before that," Peter interrupted. "The bit about carrying them round in a bag like bowling balls." He was trying to remember exactly how big the heeble-greebs had been.

"Can we go back and take a look at them again?" he asked. "And you'd better give me those sturdy gloves after all."

36

NEW AMMUNITION AGAIN

bout half an hour later, they set off walking again. The bazooka was rather heavy on Peter's back.

"We might have to slow down a bit," he said. "I can't move quite as fast with all this weight."

"I told you it was a stupid idea," said Amanda. "And everything's going to hear us coming, because of all that noise. I still think you should leave the thing behind."

But Peter wasn't going to do that. He thought it was a great idea. And the noise wasn't all that loud. The bazooka casing muffled it a lot.

"But now we've got a weapon," he said. "We'll be able to fight back."

"It's better not to have to fight in the first place," said

Amanda. "If you keep quiet, you can sneak around and nothing knows you're there. But with all that rattling going on, they'll hear us a mile away."

Peter thought Amanda was exaggerating the problem.

"You just don't like the bazooka," he said. "You never have."

Amanda had to admit that this was true. "I just don't think it's any use."

"It wasn't much use loaded with all those paintballs," Peter agreed. "But now we've changed it for better ammunition."

"Now it's heavy and noisy," said Amanda. "Big deal!"

Peter was getting angry.

"Look," he said, taking the bazooka off his back. "Can't you see all that energy in there? They're going to be very angry once they get out."

In actual fact, the ammunition looked very angry already. There inside the bazooka, where the row of paintballs had been, was a row of heeble-greebs. They were rolling around, wriggling their tentacles, trying to escape.

"It was you who gave me the idea," Peter told Amanda, "when you compared the heeble-greebs to bowling balls. And it all works so well. The heeble-greebs are exactly the right size and much more dangerous than paintballs. Uncle Bob tried to use rocks, but they were too heavy."

Amanda shook her head in exasperation.

"Boys and their toys!" she exclaimed.

"Look," said Peter, "this could save our lives..."

"Have it your own way," Amanda said, "but do me a favour and wrap the thing in this." She reached in her bag, brought out a rug, and handed it to Peter. "That should keep the noise down at least. Now can we get on?"

Peter did as she suggested and returned the bazooka to his back. It felt heavier than ever, but he thought it best not to complain any more. At least she was right. It had cut down the noise of all the protesting heeble-greebs.

Now they were on a narrow path with trees to either side. It seemed to Peter that the trees were sort of wobbling.

"Are any of these dangerous?" he asked, but Amanda told him they weren't.

"Not unless you lean against them," she said.

"What do you mean?" asked Peter.

"They're bendy trees," said Amanda. "If you lean against them, they bend right back and then they act like a catapult. They could send you flying right across the vale."

Peter ruefully shook his head. You had to keep your wits about you round here.

Then Amanda touched his arm.

"Quiet," she whispered, "there's something coming! Hide over there in the trees. But make sure you don't–"

"Lean against them," said Peter. "I know."

They went to hide amongst the trees and crouched there, peering out. Something was coming along the path ahead of them.

37

THE LIFKIN

The thing they saw on the path resembled a little old man, walking along with his eyes on the ground as though he were looking for something. As he walked, he muttered to himself beneath his breath, and shook his head in apparent dissatisfaction. But as he drew closer and Peter was able to get a better look, he saw that this "little old man" could not be human. His arms and legs were somehow too long and too spindly, and his legs looked as though they couldn't have the strength to carry his weight.

Peter remembered his grandfather, who had died when Peter was very young, but had once made Peter a model of a man. Peter's grandfather had smoked a pipe and used thin, wiry, furry things to clean it with. He'd made the body and head of the model man out of plasticine, and used the thin, wiry, furry things to serve as its arms and legs, bending them into shape at the knees and elbows.

This "little old man" on the path reminded Peter of that model, though with great, oversize, furry feet, which made his legs seem more spindly than ever, and a shock of hair like the floppy head of a mop. As he drew level with where the children were hiding, he stopped and seemed to be listening, peering around him with sharp, tiny eyes. Peter was very aware of the faint but unmistakable sound of the angry heeble-greebs at his back. Although Amanda didn't speak, he could hear her say "I told you so," in his head.

And then the 'little old man' seemed to be looking straight at them, peering through the gloom, which had now turned purple again. He reached behind his back and produced a bow and then an arrow, and cautiously crept forward towards the children.

Peter wondered if he should get the bazooka ready or just keep still. He tried to guess what Amanda might be thinking. The sound of her not breathing beside him was deafening.

Bit by bit, the 'little old man' edged forward, his tiny eyes peering over the top of his large, angular nose like two berries sitting on top of a tree. His round mouth was pursed in concentration.

Peter wondered if they should get ready to run.

But then there came a different sound from along the path the way they had come, and the 'little old man' gave a startled jump and turned to look. "*Scree!*" came the sound, "*Scree, Scree!*" – high-pitched and piercing.

The 'little old man' fired an arrow, then scurried out of sight, the "*Scree, Scree,*" sounds becoming more distant.

At Peter's side, Amanda started breathing again.

"He's chasing after that screecher," she said. "Let's get out of here,"

They crept out from among the trees and saw the 'little old man' chasing away along the path, with something that looked like a vast goose screeching and hopping beyond him.

Amanda shook her head.

"He probably won't catch it," she said. "Lifkins are lousy hunters. They'd rather barter or find things lying around."

"What are lifkins?" asked Peter.

"That was a lifkin," Amanda said. "I'll tell you about them later. For now, let's get a move on, in case he comes back."

"Would he have killed us?" Peter asked, as they

hurried along the path. The '*scree!*' sounds had died out behind them now.

"If he'd tried to shoot the arrow, he'd probably have missed," replied Amanda, "and then I'd have shown him the horn I've brought along."

"And what good would that have done?" asked Peter.

"Let's save our breath for running just now, shall we?" suggested Amanda. "I'll tell you more when we get to where we're going."

"And where's that?" asked Peter.

Amanda didn't reply.

Overhead, the sky had turned tangerine.

38

The Edge of the Hollow

Before long, they came out of the trees and the path began to climb amid wiry bushes. They slowed their pace to take the hill and Amanda began to explain about the lifkins.

"They sort of hold things together here in the vale," she said. "They see to the needs of the other creatures and keep the place neat and tidy. They pick up things that are lying around and usually find a use for them. If they can't use them themselves, they'll think of another creature that can. They're really rather clever in their way."

"So that's why we saw that lifkin before it saw us," said Peter. "It had its eyes on the ground because it was looking for what might be lying around on the path?"

"That's right," said Amanda.

"But is there really much lying around?" Peter asked. "It's not exactly busy round here, is it?"

"Not at this time of year," said Amanda, "but you should see it in season. In a few month's time, there'll be ghosts and bogeys wherever you turn."

Peter gave a shiver.

"And then there's the stuff that the tourists leave," said Amanda. "You'd be surprised what they leave behind when they panic and run off screaming. Some of the lifkins make their clothes out of sweet wrappers. And don't forget that the strangeness throws up stuff from time to time. You saw that boulder turn into a beetle back in the clearing. Well, not everything that the strangeness produces can crawl away like that. The lifkins never know what they're going to find next."

"You seem to know an awful lot about them," Peter said. "Have you come across them before when you've been in the vale?"

"Occasionally," Amanda replied with a shrug, "but most of what I know, I've read in books."

Now Peter was really intrigued. It had never occurred to him there might be books about the vale.

"Who writes them?" he asked.

"The explorers, of course," said Amanda, "but they're not widely available except to people who live in

Peculiarshire. Otherwise the tourists would know too much,"

Peter found himself getting angry again. He didn't like the way the tourists were fooled.

"The thing the books make very plain about lifkins," Amanda said, "is to bear in mind that they're in it for themselves. Like I say, they help the other creatures, but they only ever do it for a price: for some food, or something useful, or something that they might be able to barter for something else."

"Is that why you brought that horn," asked Peter, "to barter with lifkins?"

"Yes, that's right," said Amanda, looking surprised. "You're not that stupid all the time after all, are you?"

"Thanks a lot," said Peter.

"That's all right," said Amanda brightly. "The lifkins are very inquisitive, you see. They may not have seen a horn before, so I'm hoping they'll like it. Now, be quiet," she warned. "I think we're almost there."

They crested the hill and found themselves looking down into a narrow chasm at the foot of a slope ahead, with clumps of trees and bushes gathered round it. From out of the chasm's inner gloom, there came the occasional faint light or plume of blackened smoke. A few creatures which looked like lifkins were climbing in and out of the chasm, some of them holding poles and others holding torches. As the children watched, they heard a faint, ringing cry, and Peter found he could almost make sense of it. He had the feeling that if he listened just a little bit harder, he would be able to understand what it said.

"Was that a human?" he asked.

Amanda looked very thoughtful.

"Perhaps," she said. "On the other hand, it might be a lifkin as well. According to the books, they can speak our language."

Now, Peter was very surprised. "How's that?"

"It's like I said," Amanda replied, "they pick things up. Shall we see if we can get a bit closer?"

She led the way carefully down the slope, dodging behind a bush or a tree whenever a lifkin appeared. Peter followed as best he could, the bazooka banging against his back as he went along. At one point, Amanda suddenly changed direction, and Peter thought that a lifkin must have seen them.

"It's all right," whispered Amanda, when Peter asked. "Didn't you see? We were heading towards a jamjam bush. It's always best to give them a wide berth."

Peter shook his head. He should have known. He still had a lot to learn about how to stay alive in The Vale of

Strange. They were drawing close to the edge of the chasm now, and the air grew more heavy and stale. The smell reminded Peter of a dustbin.

"What's inside that chasm?" asked Peter, though part of him very much wanted not to know. "Why have you brought us here?"

"Because this is the only one I've seen," said Amanda. "There are many others, but I don't know where they are. I'd have to study the maps and there wasn't time."

"Many other *what*?" asked Peter. "What are you talking about?"

"Boggy hollows," Amanda said. "Where the bogeys live. This is the only one I've ever found. I suppose they'd be much more easy to find in winter, when all the bogeys are flying about, but I've only ever been in the vale in the summer, when it's safe. I might be daft, you see, but I'm not stupid."

"I wouldn't call this 'safe' exactly," said Peter.

"Compared to the winter, it is," said Amanda. "The bogeys and most of the other creatures are hibernating now. Except for the odd one that can't sleep."

"Like the one that carried off Algernon, you mean?"

"That's right," said Amanda. "But maybe a bit of a fly around was just what it needed to make it tired. Maybe it's down there now, sleeping it off."

"Or maybe it's not," said Peter glumly. "Maybe it's still flying around or sleeping in one of the other hollows. The ones you can't find."

"I warned you this might be a lost cause," said Amanda. "But wait...did you hear that sound?"

Peter listened and there it was: the ringing cry had come again, a little bit louder this time. But he still couldn't understand what the words meant.

"We need to get closer," said Amanda. "Follow me."

She led them around a clump of spiky bushes. Just ahead, they could see the edge of the great chasm itself and catch a glimpse of the sheer walls and many crannies within.

"Those are the holes where the bogeys live," said Amanda. "Bogey pits, they call them. They sleep in there with a pile of food to keep them through the summer."

She looked at Peter tellingly, and Peter gave a gasp.

"Do you think that Algernon—?" he began.

Then the sound they had heard before came again. Now they had come so close to the chasm, it was mixed in with other sounds: grunts and mutters, bangs and clatters, and something that sounded like snores. But now there was no mistaking the words that the distance had muffled before.

"Help! Bogeys!" somebody was shouting.

Amanda and Peter exchanged glances.

"Algernon," they whispered.

"Algernon? What is this?" came a gruff voice from behind.

And they turned to see a lifkin there, standing right beside them, peering down with suspicious eyes and holding a mighty axe.

39

THE ALGERNON AND THE HORN

"Get out the horn," whispered Peter, as they edged away from the lifkin.

"Let *me* decide how to play this, all right?" said Amanda.

The lifkin held his axe as though ready to strike a blow and looked from one child to the other.

"Not tourists," the lifkin muttered. "Both afraid but haven't run off screaming. Not explorers either, though. Too young to be explorers, surely?"

Amanda and Peter looked at each other. The lifkin seemed to be speaking his thoughts aloud.

"This Algernon," said the lifkin. "The way they said it sounded like it was valuable."

He was stroking the edge of his chin now, peering at

Amanda and Peter through narrowed eyes. He was about a foot or so taller than they were, though some of this extra height was due to his great shock of hair, which sprang from his wrinkled head like the leaves from a tree. In his eyes was a hint of greed and a twinkle of expectation.

"Oh yes," said Amanda, "it is worth a great deal. An Algernon in the land of the humans is worth as much as, oh, a sack of potatoes."

The lifkin's face fell. "Potatoes is scarce in the land of the humans?" he asked.

"No," said Amanda. "Not really."

The lifkin looked perplexed. "Then why you say this Algernon is valuable?"

"Because I happen to be very fond of potatoes," Amanda replied.

The lifkin muttered under his breath. He was trying to work this out.

"This Algernon," he said at last, "you have it in your bag?"

"No," said Amanda, "we do not have any Algernon. We are hoping to find one."

"So you do not have any Algernon to barter?" the lifkin asked.

"No," said Amanda, "we wish to barter to get it."

"Ah," said the lifkin, understanding at last. "But we do not have any Algernon here—have never even seen it. Do not even know what this Algernon look like."

Amanda gave a shrug.

"You do have an Algernon here," she said. "I can hear it."

The lifkin listened carefully. His nose began to twitch.

"I hear only bogey sounds," he insisted, "belching, snoring, snorting sounds. Only bogeys here. Only other thing here is ghosts—and ghosts is quiet when they is asleep, all comfy and undead to the world."

"And Algernon here as well," said Amanda. "There—can't you hear it?"

"*Help! Bogeys!*" Algernon's voice came faintly from out of the distance.

The lifkin seemed to understand at last. "Ah, this Algernon is a human," he said.

"That's right," said Amanda.

"This Algernon is a friend of yours?"

"No," said Amanda, "not at all. But this Algernon can be exchanged for a sack of potatoes."

The lifkin looked confused again. He seemed to be trying to work out if this Algernon was valuable or not.

"Lotsa trouble find this Algernon," he said. "That mean you have to barter big if all you want is potatoes.

You sure you rather not just barter for sack of potatoes instead? Cut out Algernon altogether—make it simple and nice?"

"You have this sack of potatoes?" Amanda asked.

The lifkin thought for a moment.

"Now I remember, no," he muttered dolefully.

"Thank goodness for that," said Amanda under her breath.

"What you say?" asked the lifkin.

"I say, in that case, we shall have to barter for Algernon after all," Amanda replied.

Algernon's cry came faintly again on a foul breeze from the hollow.

"*Help! Bogeys! Help!*"

The lifkin squinted into the hollow. "Sixty-three, seven, I think."

Amanda looked perplexed.

"Is that a price?" she asked.

"No," said the lifkin. "That is where this Algernon is. We lifkins are good at this. Always know number of beans in jar without counting, number of pebbles in hollow – stuff like that. This Algernon is sixty-three bogey pits along and seven down. Can tell that from its cry."

"Wow!" said Peter, very impressed.

The lifkin looked at him curiously.

"This 'wow' is valuable too?" he asked.

"Let's just stick to the Algernon," said Amanda. "I barter big for the Algernon, like you say."

"Get out the horn now," whispered Peter.

"Be quiet," Amanda told him. "I'm in charge."

"What is horn?" asked the lifkin.

"You don't want horn," said Amanda. "Horn is noisy. Here—look at this instead."

She brought out a paper tissue and handed it to the lifkin.

"Hmm," he said, examining it carefully. He laid down his axe and unfolded the tissue, letting it waft in the breeze.

"Could knot in corners and use as hat," he muttered, "or use for patch up suit of clothes." He looked down at the threadbare shirt and trousers he wore, already stitched with leaves and petals and part of a cereal packet. *Corn Flakes,* his shirt proclaimed, as though it were an advertisement, *enriched with vitamin C.* "Even so," the lifkin continued, "not very strong."

"Three ply," Amanda argued. "Just for men."

The lifkin shook his head. "But not for lifkins," he said. "Use for wipe up bogey mess, I suppose."

"Yes," said Amanda, "very good for that."

"Even so," the lifkin said, "have to be very small bogey. Big bogey use fifty of these. Got any more?"

Amanda shook her head.

"Algernon only small," she said. "Cannot give whole box of tissues for that."

The lifkin curled his lips.

"Only one Algernon going," he said, "and little girl, she very much like potatoes."

"This is taking too long," Peter hissed. "Get out the horn."

"Shut up!" Amanda hissed back. "The bartering's like a ritual. I've read it up in the books. You have to go through it all. I'm holding back the horn till the time is right."

"What you say about this horn?" asked the lifkin.

Amanda shook her head. "Horn too noisy. You look at this instead." And she handed him a spoon.

"Ah!" said the lifkin. "This could be used for bogey mess as well."

"Works very well," said Amanda.

"But not much better than tissue," the lifkin decided. "You barter shovel instead?"

Amanda shook her head. "Algernon only small."

"Girl very fond of potatoes," said the lifkin, standing his ground. "You want me take you to Algernon, you have to do better than that. I busy chopping wood to make new bogey scratcher here. Have to break off from doing that if I take you after the Algernon."

"All right," said Amanda. "I'll show you the horn."

The lifkin smiled. "You say it is noisy?" he asked.

"Very noisy," Amanda said. "Listen."

She brought out the horn and sounded it several times. Suddenly, two more lifkins with axes appeared from out of the undergrowth.

"Perhaps you should put the horn away," said Peter.

But the first lifkin was smiling broadly. He obviously liked the horn.

"All right," he told them. "For that noisy horn, I take you to the Algernon. We agree?"

"It's a deal," said Amanda, holding out her hand.

But the lifkin only stared at it in confusion.

"You barter fingers?" he asked.

"*Help! Bogeys!*" Algernon's cries blew faintly across from the hollow

"Need to keep fingers on ends of hands for now," said Amanda. "Is urgent you take us to Algernon."

Peter could only agree, and he hoped the boy would still be alive when they got there.

40

INTO THE HOLLOW

The lifkin Amanda had been talking to asked the newcomers to look after his axe.

"Do not barter axe," he said, handing it over, "or you get heads smashed in. I go to help these humans look for the Algernon."

The other lifkins wanted to know what this Algernon was, but the first one waved them away impatiently.

"I leave them puzzling," he told the children as he led them towards the edge of the hollow. "Keep them too busy wondering what Algernon is to bother to barter my axe. You should know what my name is, I think, since we make bargain now. Thinglifkin it is. Thing for short."

"I'm Amanda and this is Peter," Amanda told him. "*Brrr*...it's getting cold!"

"Of course it is," said Thing. "There are many bogeys here. Lifkins who work down in the hollow get icicles on their noses. Can cut in pieces and use in lemonade."

Now they had come to the very edge of the hollow and could see the two faces of rock with the great chasm between. Along the length of each face stretched row upon row of pits, in some of which could be faintly glimpsed the shape of sleeping bogeys. Peter felt like a fly approaching a network of spiders' webs. Something inside him said 'turn and run'.

"Are all the bogeys sleeping?" he asked hopefully.

"Most of them," said Thing. "Some of them maybe woken up but most of them be sleepy. They ask lifkins to scratch their backs, then go back to sleep again. Here – we must go down." He led the way down a flight of stairs which were cut into the steep face of the rock. All the time, the temperature continued to drop and the air grew increasingly smelly. Peter could hear grunts and snorts from the bogey pits to either side of the stairs.

The lifkin counted as they went. "One– two– three–"

"You speak our language very well," said Peter, doing his best to cheer himself up by thinking about something other than bogeys, "but don't you have any language of your own?"

"Lifkins not have anything of our own," Thing replied. "We only have what we barter or pick up. Your language we is picking up from your ghosts. Six– seven–

Here we is. Here is row of pits where the Algernon is."

Peter was glad they didn't have to go down any further. One row below, the staircase came to an end. Beyond that, he could see lifkins climbing about using handholds in the rock. Peter knew he should concentrate on finding Algernon and not being eaten by bogeys, but something Thing said had him puzzled.

"What do you mean by 'your ghosts'?" he asked.

"Human ghosts," said Thing, as he led the way along a narrow ledge past the bogey pits to their left. "One-two- three–" he counted again.

"The ghosts are human?" asked Peter, surprised.

"Don't make him think we're stupid," whispered Amanda. "Of course the ghosts are human."

"Why is that?" asked Peter.

He heard the familiar sharp intake of breath.

"Let's just say," Amanda replied, "that a lot of the ghosts have cameras around their necks."

"Cameras...?" Peter began. And then it hit him. "You mean to say that the ghosts in the vale are the ghosts of tourists?" he asked. "They're the ghosts of all the tourists that have died here?"

"That's right," said Amanda, "and don't tell me—you think it's all very wrong."

"Well–" Peter began, but he got no further. At that

moment, there came a terrible cry from the pit at his side, and he turned to see a bogey looking back at him.

This bogey wasn't black like the one which had taken Algernon, and Peter remembered now what Amanda had told him: that the various types of bogey had different colours. As far as Peter could tell by the gloomy light of the pit, this one was pale with dark spots. As he watched, it yawned and closed its eyes as though to sleep, probably thinking that Peter had been a dream.

"Do not startle bogeys," Thing advised him. "We do not wish to make ourselves centre of great attention. Otherwise many bogeys is waked out of their sleep, and I cannot guarantee they may not be killing."

"I wasn't trying to make myself a centre of attention," protested Peter. "I was only trying to mind my own business."

"No need for that," Thing assured him. "Thing is minding it for you. Do not be forgetting we make a bargain."

Peter didn't think it was worth the bother of trying to argue with this. He peered into the next pit and, to his relief, saw a quietly sleeping bogey. He tried to tell himself it would be all right.

"Twenty-one– twenty-two– twenty-three–" counted Thing.

"It won't be much further now," Amanda whispered—most likely to encourage Peter, but he suspected it was also to encourage herself. The cold and the smell were getting worse and Peter felt sure his nose must be turning blue. Perhaps he would have an icicle to barter before long.

"Why do the bogeys make it so cold?" he whispered to Amanda.

"It's something to do with the strangeness," she told him. "It's like the way it gets warmer after it snows."

This was new to Peter. But there again, there hadn't been much snow on Evil Island. Which was just as well, really. The crocodiles would have been able to hide in the snow drifts.

"Thirty-seven– thirty-eight– thirty-nine–" Thing was counting.

Peter peered across the gulf to the opposite face of rock, and saw a bogey emerge from one of the pits, flap its wings, and fly out of the hollow. Peter hoped that none of the bogeys closer to hand would develop such an urge to spread their wings. He peered into the next pit and saw a bogey stretching itself. He held his breath as he tiptoed by.

Looking further down the hollow, he saw a number of lights being carried by lifkins. He supposed that so far away from the sky, it would be hard to see without them, and he wondered aloud how far down the hollow went.

"Down to where the strangeness bubbles up," Amanda told him. "Down there, it's a sort of soup of normal stuff and strangeness. It's all a bit boggy, which is why they call this a boggy hollow. Some explorers have been down there, and one of them even returned, but his friends said he was never the same again. They say the strangeness can get into your bones."

Peter could see what she meant. He wasn't sure he would ever be the same again either. He'd be like Aunt Maggie and never go out of the house except on Thursdays. He mentioned this to Amanda.

"What's so different about Thursdays?" she asked.

"Nothing much," said Peter, "and on second thoughts, I think I'll stay at home on Thursdays as well."

Thing turned and told them to be quiet. Up ahead, along the ledge, was another lifkin wielding a pole.

"Snifflifkin here is bogey scratching," said Thing. "We must be quiet till bogey is gone to sleep again."

Peter watched as the lifkin worked, poking the pole into a pit and moving it back and forth to scratch a bogey. The beast itself was out of view, which perhaps was for the best, but Peter could hear its snorts of satisfaction.

"Is this what you lifkins do?" he asked. "Scratch

bogeys?"

Thing looked rather offended. He peered at Peter over the top of his nose.

"This is only one of many important lifkin duties," he said. "We see to many bogey needs and needs of other beasts. We clean out pits, give baths to bogeys, and listen to ghosts moan. Ghosts moan endlessly, so that is very big job..."

"You don't seem to give baths to bogeys often," muttered Peter, "not to judge from the smell around here,"

The lifkin shook his head.

"Mud baths we give to bogeys," he said. "Kills critters that live on their skin but don't improve the smell. There again, as we lifkins say, 'each to his own cup of tea'. The bogeys, they smell very bad, but not as bad as you humans. Humans, they have terrible pong of soap."

Snifflifkin's work was finished now. He pulled the scratching pole out of the pit and quickly tiptoed off. Thing and the children followed cautiously after.

As Peter passed, he looked in at the bogey which Snifflifkin had been scratching. It had settled back down to sleep with its tail poking out of its pit. Peter stepped across it very carefully.

"Fifty-three– fifty-four– fifty-five–" Thing counted.

"We almost there."

They heard the cry again, much closer now: "*Help! Bogeys! Help!*"

It was Algernon all right. Now they had come so close, there was no mistaking it.

Peter was getting nervous. "This is all very well," he said. "We seem to be on the right track, but how do we get Algernon off the bogey? It isn't going to just hand him over, is it?"

"Don't worry," Amanda whispered. "Thing will have an idea."

But for once, Amanda was wrong.

"...Sixty-two– sixty-three!" said Thing triumphantly, coming to a stop outside the sixty-third bogey pit along the ledge. "This is where the Algernon is. Now you give me horn."

"Er, no," said Amanda, "that isn't what we agreed. You must hand the Algernon over first."

Thing didn't look pleased.

"There you make mistake," he said. "I say I take you to Algernon, and that is what I do. I never promise I also hand him over."

Amanda looked at Peter, who shrugged his shoulders. Now that he thought about it, he suspected Thing was right. He hadn't promised to give them

Algernon, just to bring them to where he was. And that was exactly what the lifkin had done. Oh dear, they had made a big mistake.

Peter could see in Amanda's eyes that she knew this too.

"We only have your word he's here," she told Thing. "I can't see any Algernon, can you?"

"*Help! Bogeys!*"

"But little girl, she hear him," Thing folded his arms in defiance. "Now you give me horn!"

"But where is he exactly?" Amanda asked.

Thing pointed into the pit, where a large black bogey was lying, fast asleep. It gave a yawn and bared a mouth of terrible fangs, then gave a fearsome cry in its sleep and hiccupped.

"You see that bogey?" said Thing.

Amanda replied that they could hardly miss it.

"The Algernon is in bogey's food hole," said Thing.

"And where is that?" asked Amanda.

"On the other side of the bogey," said the lifkin.

Amanda and Peter exchanged glances. This was what they'd feared.

The bogey itself was almost as big as the bogey pit. To either side of the bogey were the rocky walls of the pit, with scarcely room for a mouse to squeeze by.

Amanda looked at Thing. "But we won't be able to get in there without disturbing the bogey. How can we get the Algernon?"

"Not my problem," said the lifkin with a shrug. "You give me horn!"

"You can't have the horn if we can't get the Algernon," said Amanda. "You get it for us and you shall have the horn."

Thing appeared very annoyed.

"You break bargain?" he cried. "Would not have left my axe behind if am knowing this. Would cut you in pieces, make sure Thing get horn!"

"I think it's time to get out the bazooka," Amanda whispered to Peter, though her tone suggested she was annoyed to have to say it.

"But you don't have the axe," she said to Thing. "And we ourselves are armed. There—you see?"

Peter had the bazooka at the ready.

The lifkin's eyes widened.

"Would gladly barter for that," he said, "if only you not lying, deceitful humans!"

"Our bargain is for the horn," said Amanda. "Get the Algernon for us and you shall have it."

"*Help! Bogeys!*" came Algernon's voice, and then an ominous splutter. Amanda squinted into the pit in alarm.

"What's that noise?" she asked.

"Sounds like he fall over," the lifkin replied. "Like I say, the Algernon is down in bogey's food hole, over on other side of the bogey. Bogey guard it, you see. A lifkin, he looks after it if bogey is away—one of many honourable tasks we perform."

"So what was that spluttering sound?" asked Amanda.

"Food hole full of boggy ooze," said Thing. "The Algernon, he trapped in there—bogey saving for later. The Algernon fall over in boggy ooze."

"Will he drown?" cried Peter in alarm.

"Probably not," said Thing. "Probably find his feet again and all is well. Until the bogey eat him, of course," he added.

"Help! Bogeys!" Algernon sounded more wretched than ever.

"There you are," said Thing. "Algernon live."

"But not for very much longer unless you help us," said Amanda. "What about it? Do you want the horn?"

With his arms folded and a scowl so deep his eyes nearly disappeared, the lifkin did not look happy.

"You break bargain!" he cried.

"I'm very sorry," Amanda told him. "We didn't mean to, honest! We just didn't listen closely enough to what you said. Come on, please help us. I'm sure it's very easy for you to go and get the Algernon. You work with bogeys all the time, don't you?"

"Yes," said Thing, "but relationship based on trust. Bogeys trust us guard their food. If lifkin steal bogey food, it very serious matter."

"Even so," Amanda said, "you want the horn..."

"You are evil influence!" cried Thing. "You are tempting honest lifkin to life of crime."

"But it's only a very little thing," said Amanda. "And poor Algernon's only small. He doesn't deserve to die!"

"Nor bogey deserve to have food stolen," said Thing. "No moral high ground here."

Amanda brought the horn out and showed it to the lifkin.

"Lovely noisy horn," she said. "All yours if you help us."

Thing looked at the horn and then at Peter. He must have been tempted to snatch it away, but he didn't like the look of Peter's bazooka.

He stood and thought for a moment, then gave a sigh. "All right," he said, "Thing will do it."

41
THE BOGEY PIT

As the children watched, Thinglifkin entered the pit. He went across and muttered something into the bogey's ear. It opened a sleepy eye and shuffled over to allow the lifkin to pass by at its side.

"That's right," the lifkin said, in a soft, reassuring voice. "You let me by so I can clean out pit. Very soon, the pit be clear of bogey mess again." He gave the children a wink. "It don't understand," he said, "but go by sound of voice. If I sound scared instead of calm, it very much eat me perhaps."

Amanda and Peter looked at each other. They didn't dare speak. The bogey still had one of its eyes open. Across the hollow, there came the sound of a distant bogey's cry. Overhead, the sky was turning green.

A moment later, Thing disappeared round the other side of the bogey. The creature had settled to sleep again, but its tail twitched as it dozed. Peter knew they were inches away from death. He could lean forward and reach out a hand and tickle the bogey's greasy fur, and its teeth or its claws could take him in an instant.

The bogey's body was slightly smaller than that of an adult human, but its fearsome appearance made it seem rather larger. Its face was a bit like that of a bat, but with large floppy ears, and its wings had sharp barbs on their edges like the spikes on the top of railings. By the dim, eerie light of the vale, the bogey's dark fur was the colour of midnight, tinged with a faint sheen of sickly green.

From behind the bogey, there came a squelch and then a dripping sound.

"Help...!" came the sound of Algernon's voice, but it quickly died away. Peter wanted to go and help and check that the little lad was all right, but he knew he couldn't run the risk of waking up the bogey.

Then Thinglifkin came back into view, carrying Algernon in his arms. One of his hands was over the little lad's mouth.

"Now stop that struggling," the lifkin told him calmly. "Stop that struggling or you get fed to bogey."

Algernon had been wriggling about, but now he became still, allowing Thing to squeeze safely back past the bogey.

"Here is the Algernon. Give me horn!" said Thing.

"Thank you very much," said Amanda, as Algernon broke free of the lifkin and came across to his friends, looking very relieved to see them again.

"Bogey came out of the sky..." he said, starting to tell them everything that had happened.

"Yes," said Peter, "but better be quiet just now. You can tell us about it later."

Amanda handed the horn to Thinglifkin.

"We really are grateful," she said. "I'm sorry about that little misunderstanding."

"So is I," said Thing, squeezing the horn to make it sound. It echoed very noisily through the hollow.

"Perhaps you should save that for later," Amanda suggested nervously. "You don't want to wake the bogey,"

"Yes I do," said Thing. "You break bargain. It serve you right!" And he sounded the horn again.

One of the bogey's ears twitched, and from somewhere nearby came a fearsome cry.

"No, please," said Amanda. "I'll give you something else to make it up to you. Would you like some strange tomatoes, perhaps?"

"Thing will not be bribed," said the lifkin. "Thing owe bogey favour now. Let him know his food is stealed." And he went back to the bogey and lifted a large, floppy ear.

"No!" cried Amanda and Peter together, but Thing paid them no heed. He sounded the horn right in the bogey's ear.

"Serve you humans right," he cried. "Teach you break bargain."

And the bogey yawned and stretched and saw the children.

42
STRANGE CREATURES ALL OVER THE PLACE

"Run!" cried Amanda, but Peter didn't need telling. He grabbed hold of Algernon's hand and hurtled along the narrow ledge, partly leading and partly dragging the little lad along. Behind them, Thing was sounding the horn time and time again, going from one pit to the next and sounding it in the ears of all the bogeys.

"Why did I bring that horn?" Amanda asked herself out loud. "I could have brought him any one of my old toys, couldn't I? Like tiddlywinks or the building bricks or the painting by numbers set. Why did I have to bring him something so noisy?"

"It seems to me he takes umbrage very easily," said Peter. "If only we could have sat down and talked it over a while..."

"What did you say?" called Amanda.

It wasn't easy to hold a conversation there and then. Their voices were drowned by the sound of the horn and the cries of bad-tempered bogeys, none of which were very pleased to be woken up in the middle of hibernation.

"Thieves!" they heard the distant voice of Thing. "The humans come and steal your food. Chase them!"

"And I thought we were getting along so well," muttered Peter. Then he heard a cry at his side and and felt a pull on his arm as Algernon tumbled over. He bent to help the little lad up, then glanced behind to see a bogey hurtling towards them from out of the sky, its teeth bared and its claws poised to snatch them up and carry them off to its pit. Peter dragged Algernon to his feet and pushed them both against the wall of rock which rose beside them, the dividing wall between two adjacent bogey pits. Then he called out to Amanda, who ducked as the bogey hurtled by, narrowly missing all of them and giving a great screech of frustration.

Peter spotted two more bogeys hopping along the ledge towards them, spurred on by the urgent cries of Thing. *There's only one thing for it,* he thought. *It's time to use the bazooka.*

"Don't bother with that!" cried Amanda, as Peter readied the weapon to fire. "We need to get out of here fast." And she grabbed hold of Algernon's hand and dragged him along behind her, scurrying off along the ledge, leaving Peter to face the bogeys.

"Thanks Amanda," Peter grumbled. As he lifted the weapon to take aim, the angry heeble-greebs rattled about inside. Through the sight, he could see the approaching bogeys.

The sky above had now turned yellow and, by its light, he could see that the leading bogey was covered in scarlet spots. Its eyes were fixed on Peter and it drooled as though it was thinking of taking a snack. It wasn't hard to guess what it hoped would be on the menu.

It's either it or me, thought Peter as he steadied himself and pulled the trigger. To his relief, the bazooka fired and a heeble-greeb flew towards the bogey, which opened its mouth in alarm and took the heeble-greeb on its nose, the tiny creature's teeth digging deep in the bogey's flesh. The bogey gave a cry of pain as Peter pressed the trigger again, and noticing this, it came to a halt, the unsuspecting bogey behind it smashing into its back. As the second heeble-greeb hit home, biting into the bogey's breast, the two bogeys hopped about, screeching and flapping their wings, fighting to keep their balance on the ledge.

Then Peter saw a shadow descending and threw himself down on the ground. The bogey which had attacked them first had flown in for another attempt, but once again it missed its target, flying over the top of Peter and bumping into the other bogeys. All of them now lost their balance and plunged into the chasm, flapping their wings furiously to pull themselves out of the dive.

Peter didn't wait to see any more. He got to his feet and ran along the ledge, hurtling after Amanda, hoping soon to see the stairs down which they had entered the hollow. He saw Amanda ahead of him, with Algernon at her side. He thought that she couldn't be far now from the stairs.

But then, as he watched, Amanda and Algernon lurched to a sudden halt. A bogey had blundered onto the ledge ahead of them. It had come from an adjacent pit, woken by all the noise.

"Pull back, Amanda!" cried Peter. "I'll get it with the bazooka!"

But he couldn't tell if she heard him, for a moment later, something else demanded his attention. A swarm of bogeys was heading towards them from out of the sky above the chasm, bogeys which came in all the colours

Amanda had told him about: black, white, green, and scarlet-spotted. Peter stopped and aimed the bazooka, firing it out above the chasm, the heeble-greebs homing in on their targets. As the creatures began to bite the bogeys, Peter turned and ran, trusting in the heeble-greebs to do their work.

Peter was relieved to see that Algernon and Amanda were still unharmed. The bogey which had been blocking their way was covered in some sort of foam. Thrashing blindly and screeching in pain, it toppled off the ledge, flapping its wings to save itself and screeching all the more.

"What happened?" Peter asked, as he caught up with the others.

"Mr Puddle's Unctuous Splodger," Amanda told him, putting the can away in her bag as she set off running again. "Well, it says it can be painful if you get it in the eyes.

They were almost upon the stairs now, and this encouraged Amanda and Peter to put on a spurt of speed, but Algernon was finding the going hard.

"I've had enough," he protested. "Wanna sit down!"

"Come on, Algernon!" Peter told him. "I'll give you a piggyback up the stairs."

Algernon liked the idea of this and jumped up onto

Peter's back. He felt very soggy and slimy because he was covered in boggy ooze from the bogey's food hole. He smelt extremely strongly of rotting cabbage.

"You go first," said Amanda, and Peter began to climb the stairs, the bazooka clutched in his hands and Algernon clinging on around his neck. The higher he climbed, the greater the weight of the little lad seemed to become, until at last it felt like he had a bogey on his back. Then he became aware of ominous shadows all around, but he felt that if he looked up, he would overbalance and tumble into the hollow.

Please don't let them get me, he thought, concentrating on climbing the stairs, finding the strength to take another step and then another, knowing that it couldn't be far to the top of the hollow now, but fearing at any moment he'd feel a bogey's claws upon him, trying to drag him off with it and take him away to its pit. When the last of the stairs finally came, he could hardly believe he was there. He let Algernon slide off his back and turned and looked around.

He saw that Amanda was still on the stair, throwing something small and round at a bogey hovering beside her. It seemed to be trying to get close enough to grab the girl in its claws, but it was also trying to get out of the way of whatever Amanda was throwing.

"What are you throwing?" cried Peter.

"Strange tomatoes," Amanda replied, as one of them hit the bogey on the nose with a loud wail. This gave her time to clamber up the rest of the stairs. When she got to the top, Peter reached down a hand to help her.

"They're quite good," Amanda said. "I've used them to chase off three of the bogeys already. They don't seem to like tomatoes at all."

"But you shouldn't be using them," Peter protested. "I was going to take them home for Uncle Bob."

"Don't worry, there's plenty left," said Amanda.

"Couldn't you have used the Splodger instead?"

"No," said Amanda. "The can's empty."

"Or asked me to use the bazooka?"

Amanda gave a shudder. "No, I don't like that. It's dangerous!"

Peter gave a cry of exasperation.

"And the bogeys *aren't*?" Then he saw a shadow again and looked up at the sky. "Watch out—it's coming back!"

The bogey which Amanda had hit was swooping in for another attack, followed by two more. Amanda got some tomatoes out, but Peter had the bazooka ready and saw them off with a hail of flying heeble-greebs.

"The bazooka works really well," he said, pressing the trigger one last time for luck—but then there was a strange noise and the rattling inside the bazooka grew louder. The heeble-greebs that were left inside seemed to be getting angrier than ever, and now that their companions were gone, they had a lot more space to rattle about in.

"It seems to be jammed!" cried Peter, trying again. And then there came a loud crack and the bazooka came apart in his hands, bits of plastic and heeble-greebs flying everywhere.

"Quick! run!" cried Amanda, seizing hold of Algernon and dragging him out of the way. Peter turned and ran as well and almost flung himself down on the ground, until he remembered this wasn't a good idea.

A heeble-greeb banged against his boots as he turned to check on the others.

"Are you all right?" he cried.

Amanda gave him a thumbs up and started to make her way towards him, with Algernon at her side. They had all managed to get out of the way of the heeble-greebs as they fell, and now that the creatures were down on the ground, they couldn't do any harm. All they could do was to roll around, trying in vain to bite through the children's boots.

"I told you that thing was dangerous," said Amanda.

"I hit a lot of bogeys with it," Peter protested,

inspecting the pieces of broken plastic and shaking his head sadly.

"That wouldn't have done you very much good if the heeble-greebs had got you," said Amanda. "Guns are dangerous. I thought you might have heard."

Peter was about to reply when he looked up at the sky. A new swarm of bogeys was heading their way—and now, they hardly had anything left with which to fight them off.

"What shall we do? Throw tomatoes?" asked Peter.

"I think we should run for cover," said Amanda, looking around. "You see that clump of trees over there? Let's try and make for that,"

As they set off running, Peter could hear the cries of the bogeys above. The trees seemed to be an awful long way away.

43

I SPY

When they finally reached cover, the bogeys were almost upon them. They tried to swoop to catch the children but had to swerve away because of the trees.

But even here, the children were still in danger.

"Mind the trees!" cried Amanda. "They might be bendy."

Peter poked a nearby trunk with a finger.

It didn't bend but it gave a howl – a bit like a strange tomato.

"It's all right," he told Amanda. "They're not bendy— they're noisy."

"Even so," Amanda whispered, "it's best if we try not to touch them. If we can manage to keep quiet, the bogeys might forget all about us and fly away. According to the books I've read, they aren't all that clever."

Peter hoped that the bogeys had read the same books as Amanda. But when he mentioned this, she gave a snort.

"They can't read books if they're not clever, now can they?"

"No," said Peter, "what I meant was–"

"I'm bored," said Algernon. "Wanna go home!"

"We all want to go home," said Peter, "but we have to wait till the bogeys have gone first." Peering between the trees, he could see them flying around the thicket. They didn't seem to be losing interest so far.

"Perhaps we could play a game," he suggested. "How about 'I Spy'?"

"That's boring," said Algernon.

"Try to complain more quietly, can't you?" Amanda whispered. "They'll never go away if we make so much noise."

"Let's give it a try," said Peter quietly. "I spy with my little eye something beginning with 't'."

"That's easy. Tree," Algernon whispered. "Now it's my turn. I spy with my little eye something beginning with 'b'."

"Bogey," said Peter, feeling rather depressed.

"That was lucky," said Algernon. "Now it's your turn

again."

Peter was watching the bogeys as they circled round the trees, their tails waving behind them as they went. But did there seem to be fewer now, he wondered?

Algernon was tugging at his sleeve.

"Come on, Peter. It's your turn!"

Peter tried to think, but he wasn't inspired. Apart from trees and bogeys, there wasn't much else around.

"Can you have a go, Amanda?" he asked imploringly.

To his surprise, Amanda was willing to play.

"I spy with my little eye something beginning with 't'," she whispered.

"That's easy. Tree again," said Algernon.

"Well, yes," Amanda said, "but not the tree you're thinking of."

Algernon looked confused.

"That's not how we play the game in Nuneaton," he said.

"We're playing a game called staying alive," said Amanda. "You see those trees over there?" She pointed towards some trees in the distance, across a great expanse of open space. "Those are the trees I was looking at just now," she said. "Those are the woods that Peter and I were in before, the ones where we saw our first lifkin. If we can make it over there, we should be safe for a while."

Peter looked at the open space in alarm.

"It looks like a very long way away," he said.

"It's our only chance," said Amanda. "We can't stay here forever."

Peter looked up at the sky, which had now turned tangerine again. He hadn't seen any bogeys for quite a while. And was it warming up a bit, he wondered? It was always so cold around bogeys.

"Do you think the bogeys are gone?" he asked.

"There's only one way to find out," said Amanda. "Sooner or later, we've got to get out there and risk it."

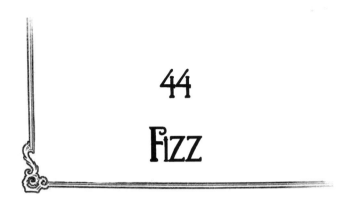

44

Fizz

"Right," said Peter, "let's pretend it's a game. I'll count down from five to one, and the first one over there wins."

"I prefer 'I Spy'," said Algernon sulkily.

"You said you were bored a moment ago," said Amanda. "Well, I don't think you're going to be bored for very much longer."

Peter looked at the sky again. Still no sign of bogeys.

"Right," he said, "here we go. Five– four– three– two– run!"

They dashed out of the thicket, hurtling across the open space, afraid at any moment to see the shadows of bogeys before them. They were holding hands, with Algernon in the middle, his legs moving frantically as he tried to keep pace.

"Chocolate cake!" cried Peter, doing his best to encourage him on. "There's ice cream in those trees over there. Apple pie and chocolate bunnies and... What's that?"

It was a humming sound from somewhere in the distance: a strange sound like a mighty swarm of bees.

"Oh no!" cried Amanda. "They're coming back."

"What?" said Peter. "The bogeys, you mean?"

"Of course I mean the bogeys. What did you think?"

"But I thought they'd gone away," Peter protested.

"Perhaps they only pretended to go. To lure us into the open."

"But I thought you said bogeys weren't very clever."

"I didn't say that," Amanda told him. "That was just the explorers who wrote the books."

"The ones that all got killed, you mean?" asked Peter.

"That's right," said Amanda.

Peter wished she'd mentioned that bit before.

The humming sound was gradually growing louder. It sounded less like bees now than aeroplanes.

"Are you sure it's bogeys?" Peter asked, as they hurtled on towards the woods. "I've not heard them sound like that before,"

"That's the sound they always make, just before it happens,"

"Just before what happens? *Oops!*"

Peter felt a tug on his arm as Algernon fell again. As he turned to help him up, he saw the bogeys heading towards them out of the orange sky.

"Oh no," Amanda cried. "He hasn't got a hat!"

"What?" said Peter. "You don't mean...?"

He looked down at Algernon, who didn't have a hat. The little lad had seen the bogeys too.

"Help! Bogeys!" Algernon cried, and started to run away in the wrong direction.

Amanda searched through her bag, then flung it at Peter and hurried away, chasing after the little lad.

"It's my fault! I should have checked he had a hat," she cried. "He's got no hat and the bogeys are going to fizz!"

Peter scurried after the others, rummaging about in the bag for a hat as he ran. But all he seemed to be able to find was tomatoes...

Overhead, the buzzing sound grew louder still. Peter saw that the bogeys were almost directly above them now. There wasn't time to find a hat for the little lad.

"Stick your hands in your pockets," came Amanda's warning shout. "Don't let the fizz touch your skin!"

And then the fizz began to fall: great dollops of pink stuff, which fell to the ground and fizzed like lemonade.

Peter could feel it falling across his shoulders and over his hat. He felt as though he was being attacked by candy floss.

Ahead of him, he could see that Amanda had flung herself down on the ground. He couldn't see any sign at all of Algernon.

He shouted the little lad's name in panic, afraid that the fizz had eaten him up altogether. After all they had done to help him, was it going to end like this?

But then he saw that Amanda was stirring and getting back to her feet. The fizz attack was over now – the bogeys were flying away. The pink stuff had dissolved, like ice in the midday sun.

As Peter reached Amanda, he saw her helping Algernon up off the ground. The little lad didn't seem to be hurt. *She must have flung herself across him to shelter him from the fizz,* thought Peter. She'd run the risk of heeble-greebs, but there hadn't been anything else she could have done.

Peter stared at Amanda in amazement.

"You saved him!" he cried and shook his head. "You aren't so bad after all!"

"I suggest you hold your compliments for later," said Amanda. "We don't have time to stand here chatting now."

"But the fizz attack is over," said Peter. "The bogeys are all gone."

"Oh no, they're not," said Amanda. She pointed up at the sky. The bogeys had turned and were coming back down towards them.

"They only use the fizz to soften up their prey," she said. "They always come back for the kill. Looks like we might have about a minute to live!"

45

Exploding Carrots

As they ran, it seemed to Peter that the woods were just as far away as ever. He could hear the cries of the bogeys behind them and didn't see how they could possibly make it in time.

"At least there won't be fizz this time," said Amanda. "They're not humming. They always hum when they fizz."

Peter didn't think this was much consolation. There might not be fizz but there would be bogey claws and jaws and those sharp barbs on the edges of their wings.

"My legs are hurting," Algernon cried. "Don't wanna run anymore!"

Peter tightened his grip on the little lad's hand.

"Not much further now," he cried. "We're almost there!"

He did his best to sound convincing, but even the little lad could see he was lying.

"Don't wanna," Algernon cried, breaking away from Peter's hand and standing his ground, folding his arms in defiance.

Peter could hardly believe it. Algernon had bolted away from imaginary bogeys often enough. Now here they were with the real ones almost upon them... He pointed into the sky in exasperation.

"Look! Bogeys!" he hollered.

The bogeys were drawing very close. The temperature was falling. Peter thought he could almost see the yellows of their eyes.

But Algernon refused to turn and look.

"My legs hurt!" he protested.

Peter turned to Amanda, who had come to a halt a short distance away.

"Can't you talk him round?" he cried, "threaten to beat him up or something like that."

But Amanda could only shrug. Something in her eyes told Peter she knew that the game was up.

"Run and save yourself!" he cried. "You don't have to wait for us."

But Amanda shook her head.

"Perhaps we can pick him up," she suggested, "carry

him between us." But her words could not disguise that look in her eyes.

Peter looked at the bogeys again and saw it was hopeless. Any moment now, it would be too late...

And then Algernon turned around and saw them, gliding down with their claws ready to snatch him away again.

"Help! Bogeys!" he cried in terror, running away at last.

"Better late than never..." muttered Amanda.

Yet Peter could see it was useless now. The bogeys were gliding down upon them with teeth bared and claws extended, only a matter of moments away from their prey.

And then the missile came from out of nowhere: a great streak of orange against the pink and green stripes of the sky, colliding with the leading bogeys and exploding in a flash of brilliant light. Several bogeys fell out of the air, to lie in charred heaps upon the ground.

Peter looked at Amanda, thinking that she must have found something useful in her bag, something that had brought about this miracle. But he saw that Amanda looked just as baffled as he was.

Then a second missile came, taking out several more of the bogeys, the rest scattering in disarray, flapping their wings and shrieking in consternation.

Peter let out a cheer. This was even better than the movies.

But what exactly *were* these missiles, he wondered?

He asked Amanda, who looked extremely thoughtful.

"It seems a bit unusual," she said, "but it looks as though they're giant exploding carrots. I wonder where they come from?"

A moment later, they found the answer, as several humans emerged from the distant woods.

"Peter, Amanda… Are you all right?"

Peter recognised the voice of Uncle Bob. He felt a great surge of relief, followed by one of fear. This was all very well for him and Amanda, but what about Algernon?

He remembered what Amanda had said about Uncle Bob and the others: "They're especially keen to see children eaten by bogeys." As far as Uncle Bob was concerned, Algernon was a tourist and fair game for the bogeys.

He turned around to see if he could find the little lad. He was standing a hundred yards away, staring in disbelief at the fallen bogeys.

"Algernon!" cried Peter, running towards him. He had to get him away to somewhere safe.

He heard Amanda behind him, shouting about something or other, but he couldn't run the risk of stopping to listen. He had to save Algernon from Uncle Bob and the adults. He had to get him somewhere they could hide.

And then, as he reached the little lad, he remembered the ploy he'd used before.

"Like a piggy-back, Algernon?" The boy happily climbed aboard and Peter ran as fast as he could, though now, the little lad seemed heavier than ever. Behind him, he heard Amanda and Uncle Bob.

I have to get him away, he thought. *After all that's happened, I can't let Algernon die!*

But it didn't seem that Peter's hopes would be rewarded, for a moment later, a bogey came upon them. It must have fled with the rest of the horde, then circled round and returned. It landed in front of them, opening its jaws and screeching in anger. Algernon screamed and Peter stood transfixed. What could he do to fight it off, without a bazooka or even a strange tomato? He put Algernon down and told him to run away and save himself. He, Peter, would try to distract the bogey. He knew he might be killed at any moment.

Then he heard a cry at his side and somebody hit the bogey with a long, stout pole.

"Take that, you bogey!" cried Uncle Bob.

The bogey snarled and flapped its wings, doing its best to get out of the way of the pole. But Uncle Bob hit it again and the bogey decided to call it a day, stumbling away and limping into the air.

Peter saw that Algernon had fallen over again. He rushed across to protect him from Uncle Bob.

"You'll have to hit me first!" he cried defiantly.

Uncle Bob looked baffled.

"What do you mean, Peter?" he asked. "Why would I want to hit you?"

"To get to the tourist, of course," said Peter. "You want to throw the tourist to the bogeys."

Uncle Bob blinked.

"No, I don't," he said.

"Yes, you do!" said Peter. "Amanda told me."

"That was all made up," said Amanda, coming to stand beside Uncle Bob. "I tried to tell you before, Peter. They won't hurt Algernon, honest."

"I don't believe you!" said Peter.

"It's the truth," Amanda insisted. "I made it all up about them wanting the tourist children to die. I made it all up to persuade you to come to the vale. At the time, it seemed like fun," she added miserably.

Peter didn't know what to think.

"How am I supposed to know when you're telling the truth?" he asked.

They were joined by Amanda's father now, who was also holding a pole.

"What's that, Amanda?" he asked. "Have you been lying again?"

Amanda gave a sigh.

"Looks like I might be in serious trouble," she muttered.

Peter stood there, holding Algernon's hand. How was he supposed to know what to do? He noticed now that Uncle Bob had tears in his eyes, but was that because the bogeys were gone and the tourist boy was still alive? Or were those tears because of something else?

"You have to trust me, Peter," he said. "I'm your Uncle Bob. I promised your mother and father I'd look after you if they died. I wouldn't hurt that little lad, I promise!"

Peter found he wanted to believe him.

"I chased that bogey away, didn't I?" Uncle Bob protested. "Why should I have done that if I wanted the boy to die?"

"You wanted to save *me*," said Peter. He didn't doubt that. But he wasn't a tourist, was he? They thought of him as a person round here, but the tourists didn't count.

"It's true that I wanted to save you," said Uncle Bob.

"When we decided that you and Amanda must have gone into the vale, we knew we had to follow you and do our best to save you." He looked at Mr. Chubb, who gave a nod.

"And it's lucky that Mr. Grimble was able to help us," said Mr. Chubb.

Uncle Bob looked a bit embarrassed at this.

"Yes," he said. "I may have misjudged that man. His peculiar carrots worked a treat, and launching 'em wasn't a problem with all those bendy trees back there to serve as catapults." He gave a wry grin and seemed to relax. "Giant exploding carrots, eh? I ask you! They'd have beaten those strange tomatoes of mine at Strange Show without any trouble at all, even if they hadn't got themselves stolen."

Peter remembered the strange tomatoes they had in Amanda's bag. He'd brought those to make up to his uncle for Algernon taking the others. For the first time, he wondered why he'd done that? Did a man who killed the children of tourists really deserve such a present? Perhaps deep down, he hadn't believed Amanda after all. Perhaps in spite of it all, he trusted his uncle.

He looked at Amanda, then back at Uncle Bob.

"You'll let him go back to his parents?" he asked.

"Yes," said Uncle Bob.

Peter turned to the little lad.

"Did you hear that?" he said. "You're going home, Algernon! What do you say to that?"

The little lad blinked and peered up at Peter. "And get to take bazooka too?" he asked.

46

MENDING THE VASE

"I know that Amanda girl is in trouble with her parents," said Aunt Maggie, "kept in her room on a diet of Brussels sprouts for a month, but it's my belief she's done us all a favour. I still don't approve of her and she almost got Peter killed, but at least she's made him aware of all the dangers around here. Which is more than some of us managed," she added, glaring at Uncle Bob.

Uncle Bob looked uncomfortable and began to study his vase closely.

"It's not exactly as good as new, but I reckon it'll do," he said. "Do you think Mr. Grimble will like it?"

He was sitting at the parlour table, surrounded by pieces of cloth and tubes of glue. Over in her easy chair, Aunt Maggie shook her head.

"I think he'd have liked it more if you hadn't broken

the vase in the first place," she said. "And what about all the others you smashed? Are you going to mend those too?"

"I'll start on those tomorrow," said Uncle Bob. "Those are the ones I smashed with the blosh, so they'll take a bit longer to fix. It might have been better if I hadn't stamped on them too."

Aunt Maggie shook her head again.

"You and your temper!" she said.

"Well I wasn't to know..." said Uncle Bob.

"I told you it wouldn't be Mr. Grimble who took your tomatoes," said Aunt Maggie. "But did you believe me? No!"

"Well there weren't any other suspects. How was I to know that it was a tourist? Ah, that reminds me," said Uncle Bob, looking across at Peter, who was sitting in the corner, listening in. "Mr. Chubb had a word with Algernon's parents today. He spoke to them on the phone. They said it came as a nice surprise to have the little lad back. They'd been told a piano had dropped on his head."

Peter was pleased to hear this. He'd seen Algernon off the previous day, in a red bus with "Nuneaton" on the front. He'd been relieved to be able to see the little lad out of Peculiarshire himself—not that he didn't trust the adults exactly.

"That's good," said Peter.

"And I want you to know I don't resent him taking the strange tomatoes. You might say it's taught me a thing or two. It's sort of brought us together, it has, me and Mr. Grimble. That's why I'm mending these vases—it's sort of symbolic, you see. They won't be exactly as good as new, but he'll look at them and see the cracks and the way they don't quite fit together and all the handles stuck on wrong, and he'll think of all the work I've put into sticking them back together again."

"And wish you'd bought him some new ones instead," said Aunt Maggie.

Uncle Bob gave a snort of exasperation.

"You just don't understand," he said. "It's male bonding, you see. He and I are going to work together from now on, put in a joint entry at next year's show. With most of my strange tomatoes gone and all his carrots exploded like that, we're going to have to forget about it for this year. But just you wait until next! With both our skills and brainpower together, we'll sweep the board at next year's show. That mantelpiece will be bulging over with cups."

Now Aunt Maggie snorted.

"I'll believe it when I see it," she said, "you two

working together! You've never trusted Mr. Grimble, not since the day you met him."

"Well, that's where you'll be surprised," said Uncle Bob. "I trust that man implicitly since he gave up all his carrots like that to help rescue Peter. And just to show how much I trust him, I've taken the lock off my study door. What do you think of that?"

Peter had found it very useful. He'd been up there already.

"Does that mean I'm allowed up there as well?" asked Aunt Maggie.

"Of course not," said Uncle Bob. "You'll only start cleaning or something. You women are always cleaning. You don't understand the importance of dust."

"I only clean in leap years," protested Aunt Maggie.

"That's what I mean," said Uncle Bob. "You're cleaning all the time!"

"Can we go up to the study now?" asked Peter. "I want to show you something."

"Nothing would please me more," said Uncle Bob, setting the vase down on the table, where it wobbled and tumbled over.

"It needs a bit more work on the base. I'll get out the hammer tomorrow," he said. "Come along then, Peter!"

47

STRANGE IDEAS

"I want to show you something, Uncle Bob," said Peter.

"Just a moment, Peter," said Uncle Bob. He was coming behind Peter up the stairs to the study with a box in his hands. "What I've got here is some cucumber plants," he said. "I thought we might plant them in the cupboard, now the tomatoes are gone. They're only ordinary, not strange, so it won't be quite as exciting, but they should make some nice enough sandwiches in a few months' time."

"Ah," said Peter, "well..."

"But first of all, Peter," said Uncle Bob, putting the box beside the cupboard and bringing out the strange stools for them to sit down on, "I think that you and I need a man-to-man talk."

"Oh?" said Peter, feeling rather worried.

"Yes," said Uncle Bob, "to clear up once and for all the business of how we go on in Peculiarshire, about the tourists and that."

"Oh, I see," said Peter.

"I can't pretend that I wasn't upset that you thought I'd feed that little lad to the bogeys. So I want to make sure you realise that we've nothing against the tourists. We'll always do our best to save any tourist we see who gets into danger..."

"Oh," said Peter, "you often save them, do you?"

"Well, not exactly," said Uncle Bob. "That's because we're not often looking—but if we were, we'd certainly try to save 'em."

"Is that supposed to make me feel better?" asked Peter.

Uncle Bob looked uncomfortable. Somehow or other, his chats with Peter never seemed to go according to plan.

"Look, Peter, what I'm trying to say is this: we don't want the tourists to suffer any more than they have to, but it's like I told you before. Some of the tourists have to die to keep the strangeness at bay. It's just the way of the world and that's that."

"Then I'd like to change the way of the world," said

Peter.

Uncle Bob laughed.

"That's all very well," he said, "but as you get older, you'll come to see that some things are possible and other things aren't. And changing the way of the world is, well, impossible."

"I don't think so," said Peter.

"It's not what you think, it's how things are that's important," said Uncle Bob. "You have to learn to accept the world as it is!"

"I don't see why," said Peter. "I don't see why we have to accept that tourists have to die—that people go up Peculiar Hill and never come back down again 'cos they're dead."

"We have to accept it because it's the only way," said Uncle Bob. "And after all, it's like I've told you, they're not people we know."

"But we could choose to get to know them!" said Peter.

"And what would be the point of that? Then we'd only get upset when they died."

"That's what I mean," said Peter.

Uncle Bob shook his head.

"I don't understand you at all," he said. "If we tried to get to know all the people we don't know, we'd have the worries of all the world on our shoulders. Think of all the people who die in the poorer countries all over the world. Do you want us to get to know them as well? To realise that they're just like us, with mothers and fathers and uncles and aunts, only then they die 'cos they haven't got enough food? Do you want us all to get upset about them dying as well?"

Peter thought for a while.

"I don't see why not," he said, "now you happen to mention it. Perhaps if we understood more about them, we'd start to make more effort to keep them alive."

"Well that's as may be," said Uncle Bob, "but you've got to understand that it's a complicated business making a difference to things like that, and Aunt Maggie and me, well, we've a shop to run."

"But I haven't!' said Peter.

"Ah yes, but you're a growing lad. You've got to go to school and learn stuff and pass exams and things like that."

"I could learn stuff to help to change the world," Peter replied. "Learn how to keep the strangeness at bay without the tourists having to die, and learn how to stop people starving because they're poor."

Uncle Bob guffawed.

"Well, you've got some strange ideas and no

mistake!" he said. "You must get them from your father's side of the family. I'm afraid it'll take more than learning to change the world the way you want. It's going to take nothing short of a miracle," And he got to his feet and went across to the cupboard. "I think we've talked quite enough nonsense for one day, young man. Let's get these cucumbers planted now, shall we?" And he opened the cupboard and gaped at what he saw, for the cupboard was full of strange tomatoes, bigger and redder and stranger than the ones that had been there before.

"Well I never!" he said, looking at Peter.

Peter was about to explain what had happened, but then decided against it. He just sat quietly and gave a smile.

"Well I never," his uncle repeated, looking on in disbelief. "How...? Where...?" He staggered back to the strange stool and sat down again.

"Well," he said, after a while, "it looks like I might have something to learn as well..."

48

UNEXPECTED COMPANY

The next day, just for something to do, Peter took a walk in the gully they had followed on their way to The Vale of Strange. He found it hard to believe that their big adventure had only been a few days ago. In fact, now he thought about it, he found it rather hard to believe it had ever happened at all. Life since then had seemed so ordinary by comparison. Even the shop on Peculiar Hill had come to seem almost dull. He began to feel sorry that Amanda had been shut away in her room on a diet of Brussels sprouts. He knew she deserved it, but even so... without her, there wasn't an awful lot to do around there.

"Oh, it's you, is it?"

When he heard the voice, Peter almost jumped out of

his sturdy boots in shock. He had thought he had been alone in the gully, but now he saw a figure emerging from out of the high weeds. For a moment, he thought it might be a lifkin or something even worse. He tensed all over and readied himself to run.

"It's only me, stupid!" said Amanda. She looked at Peter with her nose high in the air.

Peter gaped, temporarily speechless.

"I thought you might have come to see me before," Amanda told him.

"But..." Peter began.

"I know," said Amanda rather wearily. "You thought I was shut in my room on a diet of Brussels sprouts."

"Well, yes, as a matter of fact I did," said Peter.

"And so do my parents and so does everyone else," said Amanda, "so let's keep it that way, all right?"

"Er yes, okay, but how...?"

"How did I get out here?" Amanda asked. "Is that what you want to know?"

"Well, yes..."

Amanda ran a hand through her hair and looked rather pleased with herself.

"I would have thought you knew me well enough by now to guess I'd have a strategy to deal with the situation," she said. "After all, if I can cope with jamjam plants and barter with lifkins and even put up a fight against a horde of bogeys, I'm hardly going to be defeated by a lock and key, now am I?"

"Well, no, I suppose not," said Peter.

"The Strange Hotel is very old and full of secret passages, you see."

"And one of them leads out here to the gully?"

"It's not quite as convenient as that," said Amanda, "but at the back of my wardrobe, there's a secret stair which leads down to a rose bed in the garden. It's a bit prickly and you have to be careful you don't trip over the stone gnome, but apart from that, it's all very handy. And every day, my father and mother go out, you see. My father goes off on business, and on the way, he drops off my mother for one of her beauty treatments. She has one every day: either the hairdresser or the pedicure or the mud bath or the sauna or the woman who treats all the other bits that don't get treated the other days. And on the way back, he picks her up again. So, if I go out when they go out and make sure I don't come back till they're coming back..."

Peter had worked this out.

"Then no one will notice the watch-geese making a noise," he said.

Amanda gave a rather surprised smile.

"That's right," she said. "You're catching on. And Bletch is too busy to climb to my room and check on me, of course..."

"So nobody knows you're gone."

"Right again. But I have to stay here in the gully where nobody ever comes. Otherwise someone would see me and then my parents would find out and then I'd be in more trouble than ever."

"What do you do here?" asked Peter.

"Oh, just poke about," said Amanda. "It's all very dull really. I don't suppose you've got any chocolate, have you? It's just that I fancy a change from the Brussels sprouts."

"No," said Peter, "I had a bar, but I gave it to Algernon the other day when I saw him off on the bus." He smiled and remembered the little lad, clutching the bar as the bus moved out, waving at Peter happily then falling off his seat. Peter had rarely met a kid so prone to falling over. He'd been glad and a bit surprised to hear that Algernon had made it back to Nuneaton in one piece.

"I'm glad he got safely home," said Amanda, "really I am. I know what I did was wrong. I only did it because I was bored, you know."

That's no excuse, thought Peter, but he kept his mouth shut. Amanda was surely suffering enough with the sprouts.

"I've been a bit bored myself," he admitted.

Amanda suddenly brightened. "Really? Have you?"

"Er, yes," said Peter, wondering where this would lead. Then he guessed. "Oh no!" he said. "Amanda..."

Amanda had a funny look in her eyes.

"We could go back," she said. "We could go back to The Vale of Strange. We could go tomorrow. I could meet you here with some sandwiches and–"

"But why?" asked Peter. "Why should we want to go back there?"

"You know the reason," she said. "Because it's fun."

"But it's dangerous," said Peter. "We could be killed."

"That's what you said last time, but we weren't."

"Only because of Mr. Grimble's exploding carrots."

"Well, this time we'll be more careful..."

"We certainly will. We're not even going to go there!"

"But Peter, you said you were bored!"

"Not *that much* bored," said Peter, and he turned and walked away. Something inside him wanted to say 'yes', and he had to get away before it won.

"Come back, Peter!" Amanda called.

"Goodbye, Amanda," said Peter. "I'll see you another time."

"We'll go back there," Amanda shouted. "One day,

we'll go back to The Vale of Strange!"

And even though he kept on walking, Peter had a feeling she might be right.

THE END

THE REAL GRIMLY DARKWOOD

GRIMLY DARKWOOD was born in the year nineteen hundred and blinkety blonk, which was a very long time ago. In those days, things were very different from how they are today. Carts were more common than cars, mobile phones had not been invented, and if you were very lucky, the highlight of your day was to find a free plastic spaceman in a packet of corn flakes.

Grimly thought that the sights and sounds of such days were gone forever. He was therefore surprised when, while studying the night sky with his telescope, he began to observe life on a planet which had much in common with those distant days. That he could see this place so clearly was remarkable in itself. Normally, only the brilliant stars which provide such planets with light can be observed at such a distance. But Grimly found out that he could see the planet because it possessed a phenomenon called strangeness, of which he was soon to learn a great deal more.

The Shop on Peculiar Hill is the first of Grimly's accounts of life in a part of that distant planet, a vicinity known as The Vale of Strange. He is determined that more such tales will follow, in spite of attacks from mysterious 'intergalactic forces' which, he says, are trying to sabotage his telescope and clog up his ball point pen.

Grimly rarely appears in public and his place at such events is often taken by someone called Simon Ounsley, another mysterious figure who has fulfilled numerous roles in life, among them co-editor and co-founder of a long running science fiction magazine. There are even rumours that Darkwood and Ounsley are one and the same person, though they both strenuously deny 'these unfounded allegations'. Mr. Darkwood also wishes to deny that he is 'a cantankerous old goat'.

What's next...

STRANGER DAYS ON PECULIAR HILL
book two in the
VALE OF STRANGE
series

Peter returns to the Vale of Strange with his new friend Mala, hoping to find her father, the hapless explorer Augustus Flipper, who has disappeared in a sudden outbreak of strangeness. Peter and Mala are grappling with a number of difficult questions. Why is the unpleasant Percival Crow building a swimming pool even though he never takes a swim? Why have the mysterious four-foot-high bearded Australians taken against Uncle Bob? And what has produced the lights in the sky and the multicoloured bubbles of strangeness all across Mala's lawn? Peter suspects that something big is happening here, but one question is really the most important: will the reluctant Amanda decide to help them after all?

Coming in 2019
from Journey Fiction

38219651R00155

Printed in Great Britain
by Amazon